D1212250

Sandhills Dreamer

By BJ Akin

Published by Bluestockings, United States of America, 2013

DEDICATION

I would like to dedicate this book to all of my family that has gone on before me. Dad (Orville), Mom (Ida), Sonny (Brother, Ed), Wilma, Connie and Patty (sisters). I love and miss you all every day.

And especially to my children, Montana and Patrick, for believing in me and being such an inspiration through all the trials and tribulations we have faced together. My thanks to their spouses for including me in their lives and especially my grandchildren, Austin, Carly and Cheyenne, who grandma couldn't live without! I love you all to the moon and back!

Thanks to my best friends, Patty and Dorothy who read all my bits and pieces and still supported me! Ha! Love you!

Thanks to Barb D. for her editing skills and all the helpful input to make this a better story and Bev E. for reading everything I shoved into her hands.

CHAPTER 1

Bright spring sunlight beamed down on two firm denim-clad legs as they kicked and thrashed in fragrant sagebrush, pieces flying while small white moths flittered as if in tune to a soft sputtering noise. An incoherent sound was coming from a small framed individual that was rolling back and forth in the brush, looking to be tied up with an old stained, frayed lead rope.

Anger inspired April as she muttered behind the damp dirty gag in her mouth and continued to berate herself. Ooooh! I-I-I could j-just sp-sp-spit! If only I hadn't been daydreaming! I would have seen those men riding toward me! But, oh no! Not me! I have to be off in dreamland, not paying attention to anything around me! My horse could have easily out run them since they had been riding double! Why, oh why, do I always have my head in the clouds?

Continuing to struggle, April's legs were growing weaker from a body that was bruised and sore from her ordeal. Yet, her mind still wandered. As that was normal for her, the dark haired young woman dropped into the ongoing daydream of her future. Her friends at finishing school had spent their spare time doing the same thing. Well, maybe she did it just a bit more than most. Okay, a LOT more than the other girls. But, it could not be helped. She was just a dreamer! Pure and simple!

April had been riding for the better part of a week and hadn't run into any problems with anyone she had met on the trail. When she was asked where she was headed, she replied that she was going back home and people had pretty much left her alone. Of course, no one seemed to see through her disguise at all!

Who would ever think twice about questioning a young man riding all alone? They were a common sight out here in the wide open country but it wasn't safe for a young girl to be traveling alone on horseback. And that had been the whole idea, too!

*****

Riding along on the train heading to the Sandhills, April had grown restless watching the passing wide open country. She recalled her days of freedom in Dodge City, Kansas, where she had ridden for hours in the surrounding country daydreaming to her heart's content. As she was an only child, her parents let her have her way in most things, allowing her to roam the countryside and since they knew everyone in the area they had not worried about her safety. When her mother became ill and passed away, things changed. April's father was devastated as much as she was and after a few weeks of heavily disputed conversations, he convinced her that to be a "young lady", she needed to further her education. Somehow knowing he was right, she finally agreed and begin looking forward to the trip and seeing what city life had to offer. Of course it was the start of a great adventure, giving her even more to daydream about! All too soon, she said goodbye to her father and boarded the East bound train, tearful yet excited to be traveling on her own.

Upon arriving in Philadelphia she went straight to the finishing school her father had contacted and settled in. Making friends easily, she enthralled them with the stories of her experiences of living in the "wild west". The other girls were all from surrounding towns and cities and had never been to the "wild west", let alone allowed to do some of the things that April's freedom had allowed her to do.

The flip side of the coin was that most of her new friends had male acquaintances or even a beau and it seemed that all they wanted to talk about was "it". April had no experience with men at all, so she was at a loss on what they were all gossiping about.

Listening intently and not wanting to appear unknowing about what "it" was, April would just nod her head and murmur agreement. As time went on, she realized she still had no idea! When a couple of the girls asked if she would like to meet some of the young men that they knew and attend a social event together, she readily accepted. After the Sunday afternoon picnic her partner, a bold young man, had grabbed and pulled her behind a tree and quickly kissed her. She was surprised but she didn't feel any change. That evening she looked in the mirror to see if there would be an indication of "it" on her face. Nothing. So she forgot about such things as boys for a time and studied harder, soaking up new information about the world. At least she did when she wasn't daydreaming! Watching and listening to the other girls she was fueled with thoughts of "her" dream man. Her friends talked incessantly about the lives they were planning, the handsome aspiring men they would marry and which big city they wanted to live in.

April knew she would be happier living out West in the wide open spaces, but that didn't mean there weren't handsome wealthy men there. No, she would find what she was looking for when she returned to her father's house in the Sandhills. Over the next couple of years an unrecognized yearning grew in April, one she didn't recognize.

Upon her graduation she headed home, looking forward to seeing her father and returning to the "wild west" as her friends had called it. She was determined to find a perfect "dream man" for her future husband and now she could daydream all she wanted.

That brought her to a decision. At the next train stop, she would turn in her train ticket and ride on horseback the rest of the way home! According to the map her father had drawn and sent her recently, it should only take her a few days of steady riding to reach Brewster. At Wood River, she disembarked the smoky, ash laden train, found the local Livery and purchased a horse, saddle and necessary tack. Next, she went to the General Store for men's denim pants, work shirt, jacket, boots and a large floppy hat to complete her disguise. She also purchased some food items, canteen, bedroll, saddle bags and a small skillet for her trip home. Knowing how far the trip home would be, she didn't expect to go without being prepared to eat or sleep comfortably!

That night in Wood River, April stayed in a small boarding house run by a friendly widowed woman. Early the next morning, she rose and dressed in the new duds, stuffed her long hair up under the hat and went downstairs to say goodbye.

The owner, Mrs. Douglas, was preparing breakfast when April stepped into the kitchen. When Mrs. Douglas turned from the cook stove to greet the newcomer, her smile faded slightly as she looked at the youth in front of her. She did not recall renting a room to this young man the previous night. As she started to ask if she could help him, the youth spoke.

"Good morning, Mrs. Douglas. It certainly does smell delicious in here!" April was savoring the wonderful aromas that filled the kitchen. "It smells just like when my mother used to cook breakfast for us!"

Hearing the voice, Mrs. Douglas laughed, and greeted April.

"Why, you certainly sound like that young girl that I spoke with last night. But heavens honey…what did you do with her?"

"I traded her in on a new traveling companion!" April laughed, enjoying the banter and knowing now that her disguise would work.

However, she would have to talk deeper to make it complete.

Mrs. Douglas walked over and impulsively hugged the girl. "Lordy, Miss April, I do hope you know what you are doing!"

The previous evening over supper, April had outlined her plans to the woman, feeling an instant kinship and wanting to reassure the kind woman that she would be safe traveling alone through the rough country.

"I'll be fine". April said in a slightly lower and slower voice. They both burst out laughing! "I guess I'll have to practice or try not to talk much!" April drawled.

The pair talked over breakfast and it was soon time for April to depart. They hugged and said their goodbyes, and April promised that she would write to let Mrs. Douglas know that she had arrived home safely at Brewster. As April stepped out of the boarding house into a clear spring morning, she eagerly looked forward to this new adventure and seeing her father after all these years.

Why, that seemed like just yesterday! April came back to the present and struggled ineffectively against the rope. She figured she had been only a day or two's ride from Brewster when she had been attacked by those two horse thieves. She hadn't even heard them or seen them until they were dragging her from the back of her horse. By then it was too late.

Neither one of the foul smelling men had uttered a word and in the blink of an eye, she was bound, gagged, and pummeled without even getting a chance to scream for help. The robbing skunks had tossed her into this patch of wild sagebrush, leaving her to watch as they rode off with one of the scoundrels riding *her* horse!

At first, she was totally flabbergasted. It had all happened so fast, before she even had time to react, let alone think! Now, here she was! Laying in this brush like a trussed-up Thanksgiving Turkey! Well, at least it smells good, thought April as she drew in a deep breath of the fragrant wild sagebrush. The new grass coming up was like velvet and she was glad that it was cushioning her bruised bottom!

April had spent a fretful night trying to catch bits of rest. Even though it was now the beginning of spring in the Sandhills the nighttime temperatures dropped requiring blankets or heavier clothing to keep the chill off. As soon as she would drop off to sleep, she would start awake, remember her predicament and become mad all over again. Her anger caused her to struggle against the confining ropes, and then she'd spend a few minutes of berating herself for her continual daydreaming and not paying any attention to her surroundings. For all that night and half of the next day had passed without anyone coming along to help her. She was getting almighty thirsty and hungry too!

Now, this is getting down right unsettling, thought April. Why, I could just die of thirst or be attacked by wild animals if someone doesn't find me pretty soon.   April glanced around hesitantly at the small hollow that was filled with the thick sagebrush that seemed to hold her captive. As the day wore on, she was glad it wasn't late summer.   Then, she would have had sandburs sticking in her backside and a haze of heat with dried up dust sticking in her throat.

Okay, she thought, that's it! I have just got to do something! Maybe I can holler for help. She tried rolling her sandpaper dry, swollen tongue around her parched mouth, creating just a tad of saliva but the gag was too tight. She attempted a holler but what came out was a funny sound, not too unlike a mouse being squished!

Well, that sure didn't produce much sound, she thought as panic lightly flicked through her mind.   If I could get this blasted thing out of my mouth, then I can scream for help.   Levering her feet into the bottom of a sagebrush, April pulled herself upright into a semi-sitting position. Leaning forward, she rubbed her face against her denim clad knees, snagging just a little part of the corner of the cloth from her mouth. She was so excited that she gave a couple of weak sounding yells. But they hadn't been very loud and probably wouldn't even raise a dead snake!

It was hard to believe it had been only the day before that she had been riding along, not bothering anyone, just contemplating her future. Okay, daydreaming! She had been thinking of her dream man, the future love of her life and what he would be like.

Sighing with thoughtful anticipation, April was once again off into her own little dream world.....the man would be tall, dark and handsome of course! With startling blue eyes, curly black hair and a strong commanding profile. He would be a true southern style gentleman, with upstanding character, wit, charm and of course he would have more than adequate financial means and status! He would be tall and muscular, able to sweep her off her feet, up into his arms and carry her away!

Oh....she inhaled deeply, realizing that she was somewhat breathless, just visualizing the man in her mind! Heavens! That ought to be *some man*, when I do find him! Then, unconsciously she dropped right back into her daydream.

Why, her man would make any girl limp and quivering, he would be like a knight in shining armor....her mind creating vivid images as it wandered, a charging white steed...gleaming metal. With her eyes closed, she imagined that she could feel the touch of his strong hands caressing her face as he leaned down to softly kiss her lips, running his thumb across her cheek and murmuring sweet words. He would draw her body close to his, kissing her and ..and...and...

For even with her lack of experience, she was pretty sure there had to be more than just that! Oh, she had been kissed before, by one of the young men at school, but that was all. And it had been youthful fumbling kisses; the boy's attempted groping, her slapping him soundly and loud grumbling on his part. Even then, she had silently shared his frustrations. But after that incident, the young man had kept his distance, so there were no further opportunities to find out what was to follow. And to say the least, curiosity seemed to really be her worst enemy. Of course, that was next to the daydreaming!

Oh, but there sure ought to be more to it, she thought sighing in almost defeat. Shouldn't she have felt at least some change of emotion, some enormous difference?

The other girls at school had all talked about 'it'. So why, for whatever 'it' was, hadn't 'it' happened to her? Becoming agitated, she sucked in a lungful of the fragrant air and told herself, "It will when I meet the right man! My gentleman! My future!" There, she smiled to herself, maybe some positive thinking would help bring it about!

A rustling sound emerged somewhere behind her, bringing her rushing back out of her daydream. Holding herself so still, closing her eyes, she tried to become one with the land. What was that? Holding her breath, she was positive that she had heard something that was not of her doing.

Silence.

No, it must have been just her wishful thinking. Once again she twisted her body and kicked her booted feet trying to loosen her bonds, rolling around in the brush and still not making much headway.

Ohh...hold on, there it was again! She started to holler, got half a smothered yelp out and thought, *Oh no!* What if the horse thieves were coming back? I've got to get loose and get away before they get here! Pulling against the rope that held her arms prisoner behind her, she strained to loosen it just a little more...

Abruptly, hands pulled loose the gag and were loosening the ropes on her bound wrists. Panic hit April like a ton of bricks. She let loose with a scream as loud as she could, which wasn't much considering she hadn't had anything to drink for a very long while. Kicking and thrashing around, April hoped she could somehow give whoever was behind her second thoughts about doing her any harm. She was determined not to give up, at least not without a fight!

She felt strong hands holding her still, even though she was still trying to kick loose from the ropes holding her legs and feet together. The iron strength in those hands felt firm but gentle as they tugged the ropes the rest of the way from her hands and released her. Crab-like, she scooted away a foot or so. She began fumbling with the bonds from her legs and feet, but her hands were numb and tingling from lack of use.

After a minute, even though it felt like a lifetime, she was free from the rope. She scrambled to stand up, but was wobbly, her legs weak from the prone position on the ground for so many hours. Just as she felt like she was going to fall back to the sandy ground, those same strong hands were there to hold her upright. After a few moments, she was able to stand up without help. Wondering whether her rescuer was friend or foe, she squinted up against the bright sunshine, almost afraid to look at the rest of the body that was attached to those large and yes, very interesting hands. For at this moment, one of them was holding out a canteen!

Mumbling her thanks, April greedily took the canteen, taking a long pull of cool water. Whew! She had never really known what it was to be so desperately thirsty and now, so desperately alive!

Without even thinking, she tilted back her head, and found herself peering up into the greenest eyes she had ever seen, forgetting ab-so-lute-ly everything.

CHAPTER 2

As the rugged blonde-haired cowboy topped the ridge just beyond the river bend, he thought he heard a strange sound that did not fit in with the surrounding landscape. Patrick gently pulled up on the reins of his black thoroughbred stallion, Dew Bars. Together, they paused and listened intently. The magnificent stallion's ears were pricked forward in rapt attention, just as his rider tilted his head in the same direction.

Yes, they both had heard the first sound, but waited silently listening for more. And once again, there came a muffled kind of noise. As Patrick loosened the big stallions' reins, the pair bounded forward in that direction. Even as a slight breeze cut off parts of the sound, it was getting louder as the cowboy urged Dew Bars onward. When they gained the top of the next sandhill, the pair gazed down into a small pocket of wild sagebrush and soap weed, seeing what had been creating the sounds that had lead them here.

The noise was coming from what appeared to be a youth, bound up with rope, thrashing around in the sagebrush. As they watched, the figure rolled face first into the brush, grunting and kicking, then flopping back onto his backside. Sticking his feet into a sturdy bush, the lad pulled up into a semi-upright position. As the cowboy rode down the hill, he was downwind and out of sight of the young man on the ground, making a silent approach. When

Patrick was within about twenty feet, he now could see the lad was partially muzzled, but still fighting against the ropes and emitting muffled yelps of frustration.

The kid neither saw nor heard as the green-eyed cowboy quietly stepped down from his saddle. But when the rider pulled the dirty gag from the kid's mouth, all hell seemed to break loose!

Good Gawd! Patrick thought, it sounded like the kid was being scalped!

"Hey, hold on there, rascal? I'm not going to hurt you. Just let me get these ropes off and you can tell me. How in Heaven's name did you wind up out here, hog-tied like this?"

Reaching for the arm of the kid, the cowboy helped him up onto his feet, noticing there sure wasn't much to this scruffy youth. Deftly, Patrick tugged the old halter rope from the kid's hands and feet, but the youth yanked back away from him and almost fell into the sagebrush. Grabbing onto his arm, Patrick held on a few moments till the kid was able to stand on his own. Swaying slightly the youth dusted his pants off, tugged his hat even lower down over his eyes without responding.

Patrick waited, holding out his canteen for the kid to take a drink of water. "Well, you want to tell me what happened here?"

After a long pull at the canteen, the kid quickly tipped his head up just enough to sneak a peek at Patrick and put it down just as fast. It appeared he had either lost his voice or swallowed his tongue. Time drug on for a few moments longer with nothing forthcoming. "You got a name, kid?"

Keeping his head down, the youth shuffled his small booted feet in the sand and mumbled, "Chuck".

"Chuck, what?" Patrick inquired, looking closer at the dusty but new clothes and trying to place the age of the kid and wondering where his home might be.

"Just Chuck," the kid mumbled, still keeping his head tilted down. Looking at his boots that shifted in the sand and moving his weight from one foot to the other.

"Okay, Chuck", Patrick responded shaking his head, wondering what had happened to the youth to be put in such a predicament. "Now, how 'bout you telling me, why and how you got all tied up out here in the middle of the Sandhills?"

Still the youth refused to speak. They both stood silent, not moving and neither uttering a sound. Meadowlarks sang as the wind blew the fragrant smell of spring grass and damp earth through the low pocket of brush that they stood in.

Finally, Patrick's patience won out. The kid spoke without raising his head. "I was riding through this draw and was attacked by two outlaws. They were riding double. Then they stole m-my horse, tied me up and threw me into the brush and left me here to d-die!"

"Did you know 'em, Chuck?" Patrick queried. Trying to draw the story out of the reluctant boy.

"Nope, I'd never seen 'em before, but I'll know them if I see 'em a-again. And believe me, I'm gonna find them and get my horse back, those no good skunks!" The youth raged on in a voice that was now steadily climbing a vocal ladder.

Wanting to get the story right, Patrick continued probing. "Okay, hold on now. How about you just tell me first what you're doing out here all alone in the first place. Why, you can't be more than 13 or 14 years old!"

Patrick looked at the small stature of the young boy, noticing the kid's hair looked like it had been shoved up under the floppy hat. Maybe he was just in bad need of a haircut and didn't want others to know. The hat was still pulled as low as he could get it without covering up his eyes, and such a nice warm brown they were, he mused. The boy's dusty denim pants were slightly snug over a nicely rounded bottom. His legs---hey now, wait a cotton-picking' minute!

Patrick's thoughts came to a screeching halt as he stepped back and took a much closer, intense look at the youth. Somehow, something just didn't add up here, he thought. His eyes drifted from the floppy hat down to the small shoulders to the curious swells in the top of the kid's shirt. Those had to be the strangest chest muscles he'd ever seen. Letting his eyes drift lower, he now noticed how the small waist curved out slightly into narrow hips. Suddenly, it hit him!!!

"Now wait a dog-gone minute here! Hell, you ain't no boy! You're a dang girl!"

That did it! The kid's head snapped up, as he/she stamped a small booted heel in the sand and yelled, "I am *not* a girl! I am a WOMAN!"

Patrick reached down and grabbed the old hat off the kid's head and almost passed out! For as he pulled the hat free from her head, satin hair the color of midnight cascaded out and down past her shoulders.

"There's no way in hell your name is Chuck!" Patrick growled. Never had he seen such hair. It was black as midnight, radiant with lights and shadows glinting at him as it bounced and flew in the wind.

The girl tried to pull it all back together, but the wind was in control of it now. Escaping strands flew around her like a halo, dancing in the air, defying her attempts to grasp control of it again.

"Leave it." Patrick said, slowly stepping toward the girl, mesmerized by the mass of ebony hair, as it flowed and danced around the girl's upper body. His own imagination was taking over, for in his mind he was seeing it in moonlight, spread out over the pillow in his bed...

Hey! Wait just a minute, what in the hell was happening to him? But he just couldn't help himself. He wanted to run his hands through it feel its softness, inhale its scent. He gazed down at her, arching one eyebrow and trying to frown. He saw that her eyes were now deep brown, like swirling dark chocolate. Under the layer of dirt smears on her face, she had an appealing turned up nose, covered in freckles, with high cheekbones, and lips the color of succulent strawberries, just begging to be kissed.

Unaware of what he was doing, Patrick had reached out and cupped her cheek gently with his rugged hand. She didn't move; he couldn't move. Both stood as if made of stone, caught in time. Kissing her was all he could think of at this moment.

Don't, she uttered in her mind, but deep inside she was ready to burst! She *wanted* him to touch her. She felt the heat of his gaze on her, the touch of his hand cooling her flushed face. Her lips tingled--for what? She knew not. Tension sucked the air from her lungs as she struggled to breathe. Gazing up into his darkening green eyes, April felt like she was spiraling down a long dark tunnel. Never, had she felt anything like this!

Oh my! Is this what all the girls had been talking about? Was this 'it'? She didn't seem to be able to move a muscle. Her brown eyes were welded to his piercing green eyes, unable to pull away and bring her mind back to reality.

After what seemed like an eternity, Patrick dropped his hand from her face, stepped back and quietly said, "Sorry, I didn't mean to frighten you."

The sudden loss of his touch brought April back to her senses. She dipped her head once again, "I-I don't scare easy. But, who *are* you?"

Shaking his head and trying to recollect his own thoughts, Patrick unexpectedly laughed. "Nope, I asked you first! Where did you come from and just where in heck are you headed? It's almost a two day ride to the closest town and that's Brewster, if you're going west. And dang near that far back down to Burwell, going back East. So, I'm guessing that you must be lost."

"No, I am *NOT LOST!*" she snapped, stomping her booted feet again. "I know exactly where I am and where I'm headed!"

Looking her over from top to bottom, Patrick shook his head, wondering why he was even trying to find out. "Well, are you going to tell me who you really are and where in hell you're going, or do I have to drag it out of you? Chuck?" he added sardonically.

"I'm on my way home to live with my father, *NOT* that it's *any* business of yours!" She flung back at him.

Patrick never could back down from a challenge. "Well then, let's just say that I'm making it *MY* business! Now, where does your father live and what's your *real* name?"

Putting her hands on her small hips, April scowled at Patrick, "You don't need to know who I am or where I'm going!"

"Oh, yeah? Then tell me, little missy, just how in hell are you gonna get there? Walk?"

"I can walk if I want to. I know where I'm headed!" said April, her voice increasing in volume, as she stomped the ground in frustration with his cowboy! Just who in heck did he think he was, questioning her like this, anyway?

"That does it! Now look here, little sister! You better be telling me, before I turn you over my knee and give you what for!" Now his voice was matching hers in volume. And for some crazy reason, he knew he was looking for any excuse to touch her again.

"You wouldn't dare!" She yelled right back at him, stepping forward, intending to pass him by. But just as she stomped by him, hair flying everywhere, he dropped down to one knee, grabbed her by the arm and pulled her over his knee. Even as she struggled, he popped her repeatedly on her behind. And what a mighty fine little behind it was he unconsciously thought to himself.

Infuriated, embarrassed and feeling completely off kilter, April kicked and screamed at him to let her go or she'd tell her father!

So, with a last swat to her bottom for good measure, Patrick turned her loose. "Go ahead, but you *will* tell me who your father is or I'll do it again!"

As she rubbed her smarting bottom, she glared at him, thinking he surely wouldn't be that

bullish!   The spanking had hurt more than her
bottom; it had injured her pride. It also reminded her
of the numerous times as a young girl she had gotten
into trouble and received a spanking from her father
for her efforts.   She sorely wished her father were
here now to handle this bully!   Well, she would just
show this saddle bum!

"He's Sheriff Austin Hayes, in Brewster!
And he is certainly not going to take kindly to you
manhandling his daughter!"

"Manhandling? Honey, you don't have the
slightest idea what manhandling is!   Why, I ought to
paddle your fanny again, just for good measure!
Just, how in the world could you be so naïve, as to
think you, a mere girl, could ride across country?
Out here in the Sandhills alone, no less?"

Snorting,   unladylike in   response, April
retorted. "I done told you.   I am not a girl, I AM A
WOMAN!" So much for her finishing school, she
thought, as she glared back at the cowboy who was
thoroughly irritating her.

Patrick rubbed his hand over his face.   This
girl was really starting to make him mad!   She was
sassy as hell, but she did not even realize what
danger she had put herself in.   Heaven only knows
what might have happened to her if those horse
thieves had realized that she wasn't a boy!   Never
before had Patrick been so irritated at a female in his
life.   Through a fog of anger, he heard her speaking,
but not clearly. "What did you say?"

April repeated her words to him, giving him a contemptuous look, "My father will deal with you when I get home!"

Now, it was starting to come together for him…."So you mean to say that Sheriff Hayes is your father? But, he said you were supposed to be arriving later this week on the train over at Dunning! Why, in hell, aren't you on the train that he thinks you're on?"

"Because! I was tired of all the noise and smoke! I needed the fresh air, some time to myself and to r-r-ride a horse again," she stuttered, watching the rising fury in his face. His eyes were now a very deep emerald green, like shattered glass, as they danced with jagged light. "I-I_I j-just wanted some f-freedom! S-So, I traded in my train ticket and bought a horse in Wood River and headed for home!"

Then, recovering her own anger, she erupted. "And I was doing just fine till yesterday, when they stole my blasted horse! And now y-y-you!" Indignation was pushing her to the limits of frustration.

Stubbornness not allowing her to back down, she glared into his eyes. My, they're such expressive eyes, they almost look like they are smoldering….hmmm…

"You'll think, you!" Patrick hollered right back, not knowing she was off in dreamland. "What's your blasted name? I can't call you Chuck!

And you're damn lucky those horse thieves didn't find out you were a girl, let alone the Sheriff's daughter!"

When she didn't sass back at him, he looked closer into her eyes. They were dark and swirling. She was gazing so dreamily up at him, it was as if she hadn't heard a single word he had said! Reaching out, he took her limp arm in his large hand, which immediately brought her right back to the here and now.

"W-what? I-I didn't hear you?" April stammered, knowing she had been day dreaming once again. Sometimes, she wondered if there might actually be something wrong with her. She could go off into dreamland over anything! But, *how* in Heaven's name could she daydream in this mess?

Patrick once again asked the question, "You were going to tell me your name?" Maybe, he could just paddle her into giving it to him. Yeah, now that would certainly be entertaining, he thought as he smiled to himself.

"Oh, yes, that." April tried to pull her meandering thoughts together and think! "I told you, I am a woman, NOT a girl! And my name is April, April Hayes!"

"Does your father know you pulled this foolish little girl stunt?" he asked as he reined in his meandering thoughts, even as delightful as they might be!

Frowning up at him, she continued, "well....not exactly, but I did send him a telegram from Wood River, saying I would be a few days late in arriving. I wanted to surprise him." April's voice trailed off as the realization of what could have happened if the horse thieves had found out she was a girl finally hit her full force. Out of the blue, she felt weak and light headed all at once. Maybe it was fear and maybe it was because she hadn't eaten since yesterday morning, she thought as she started to crumple to the ground. Then, she felt the strong arms of the cowboy as he bent and swept her up into his arms, bringing their faces within inches of each other. Fog clouded her mind as the last thing she remembered was flashing green eyes and the weightless feeling of floating.

Great! Now what? Patrick stood holding the girl effortlessly in his arms, looking at the surrounding landscape. Man, this day was becoming a total disaster, he thought, whistling for his stallion, Dew Bars to come to him.

The gleaming black horse trotted over and nuzzled April's cascading hair hanging over his master's arm. Dew Bars nickered softly, entreating the motionless form to move, but received no response. Muttering and shaking his head, the cowboy mounted up, holding the girl securely and headed the big stallion north.

Patrick knew that riding double he would be unable to make Brewster in less than a day and a half riding, so he figured he had best head for the line shack up on the North Loup River. It was the only shelter that was close, just a few miles away. The ranch hands stayed there when they worked cattle in the spring on the northern part of the ranch. Although the branding was done for the spring season and the cabin would be empty, there would be supplies handy. The rule of the west was to always keep wood and supplies stocked for anyone who needed food or shelter in any type of weather.

As Dew Bars walked northward at a ground eating pace, Patrick began wondering what he had gotten himself into. He was supposed to be out looking for his father's killers, not rescuing some little hot-headed girl!

Ah, but what a handful she was! Fiery tempered and downright beautiful when she was riled! He had noticed how she seemed to light up when she got mad. She sure had been a sight to watch. Why, he could stand to look at her all day long. Wait a minute here! What did he want with a danged female anyway? He was done with women!

A few years ago, he had made a promise to himself that he would never get close to another female again. Not after he had been jilted by one for a carpet bagger! But, that now seemed to be a lifetime ago. And this was the here and now. Thoughtfully, Patrick gazed down at the girl lying unconscious in his arms. Nope! No way! No how! Besides, he had other things more important to take care of.

Maybe he could leave her at the cabin, while he rode on into Brewster for her father, Sheriff

Hayes. No, he couldn't leave her alone there as it wouldn't be safe because of the horse thieving, back shooting bastards that had killed his father! He would have to take her with him now or stay at the cabin until she recovered enough to ride.

Boy! Howdy! His day sure hadn't started out with this mess in mind!

CHAPTER 3

As they continued riding northward, Patrick held the girl sprawled across his lap, softly cradled in his arms and let his mind wander back over the tragic events of the last few days.

Patrick's father, Orville Diamond, had recently died under mysterious circumstances on his way home from Brewster. He had been returning to the ranch after sending Patrick a telegram and visiting the land office.

Patrick had traveled down to Texas to purchase some herd bulls for their ranch. He had only been there a couple of days when he received the telegram from Sheriff Hayes, "RETURN HOME, YOUR FATHER WAS SHOT". But when he arrived three days later, his father had already been buried. He had been shot in the back and robbed of papers to the ranch. No one in Brewster seemed to know who had shot and robbed him or even why.

When he disembarked from the train, the local banker, Jack Monroe, had met him at the station in Dunning with an extra saddle horse in tow. After explaining what had happened to Patrick's father, the pair rode back to Brewster. By the time they arrived in front of the bank, it was mid-afternoon. Inviting Patrick into his office, Jack continued the story. "We were hit by who we think might be the Doc Middleton gang. It may have been the same day your father was killed. We're not sure. The outlaws took everything in the back safe, but they missed the one in the side room."

As they entered the banker's office, Patrick scanned the room looking at the damage to the wall by the safe. Two nice round bullet holes showed how close they had come to someone's head. "What makes you think it was Doc Middleton?" inquired Patrick.

Sitting down in his chair behind his desk, Jack said, "The guy giving the orders looked a lot like him. I just couldn't see his face clearly, with the mask and all. We figured there were six of them, four came inside and two stayed outback with the horses. They pistol whipped the front clerk, drug him back here to the safe, threatening to kill him if I didn't open it and give them all the money! I did what they told me to. I didn't want any bloodshed! Not on my hands!"

"Patrick, I sure am glad that I listened to you and your father about not keeping so much cash in this safe. Putting that extra safe in the storage room was a great idea. The robbers had no idea that it was there. Otherwise, they would have cleaned us out!"

"Did you recognize any of them?" Patrick asked, shifting his rifle, setting it down against the wall and sitting heavily into a chair. Still coming to grips with the fact that his father was now gone, he felt a bone deep sense of loss. Wishing he had been here to protect his father instead of in Texas.

"Patrick, there was one other thing I needed to tell you, just in case" the banker said, interrupting Patrick's own depressing thoughts. "Recently, your father had discussed buying the land south of your place, combining it on one deed and was intending to put it all in your name. But, son, I don't know if he made to the Courthouse to register it before he left town that day or not. If he didn't, then someone else now has those papers. Sheriff Hayes said nothing was found on your father.   No money, papers, guns, nothing. I am so sorry to have to tell you all this on top of losing your father."

"Gawd Almighty", Patrick uttered as he blew out his breath. "Can you give me the descriptions of any of the gang members?"

"None of them looked familiar, except the one guy that was dressed like Doc Middleton. Hell, I never even heard tell of Doc robbing any banks before this, let alone back shooting anyone! It just doesn't make any sense! He always took livestock and sold it.   Too bad he didn't just stay in the business and keep running the Saloon here.   I thought he had a good thing going with that. You know he was always a congenial sort. I wonder whatever made him go the route of rustling, anyway?"

Patrick, even though his mind was going in several directions, didn't want the banker to get side-tracked on telling stories of Doc Middleton and his high jinks that he was so well known for in the area. So he prodded, "Did the sheriff round up a posse and go after them?" Wiping his hand over his eyes,

Patrick tried to collect his thoughts and make plans on what he needed to do next. Talking with the Sheriff was first on the list.

The Sheriff, Austin Hayes, had been in town a few years and   Patrick knew he was a widower. With a daughter in her teens, who was back East at a boarding school or some such arrangement. No one in town had ever met her and the sheriff never talked about her all that much. At least, he hadn't to him.

Jack continued, "By the time the Sheriff rounded up about a dozen men, the robbers had at least a half hour head start. They were headed north from Brewster. It all happened late in the afternoon, so there wasn't much time to track them before dark. Sheriff Hayes said it looked like they had crossed at the Calamus River and were headed west. It was just after sundown when he and the posse reached the river, so they bedded down and planned to head out the next morning. But, during the night a sandstorm had wiped out any tracks the gang may have left. The Sheriff and posse spent half a day trying to pick up any sign of the gang to follow, but to no avail. They returned to Brewster later that day and he sent a telegram up to the sheriff at Valentine, in case they were headed up in that direction. Sheriff Hayes left yesterday morning to ride down to the Guggenmos River Ranch, to see if they had seen any strangers around their parts recently."

He was speaking of Patty and Larry Guggenmos, a young couple that had a large ranch straight east of Brewster a few miles. Larry's family had been in the Sandhills for a couple generations already. They had fought with Mother Nature and the elements, carving out a life and raising their family. They had made lifelong friends with some of the Indians, like Patrick and his family had. They all depended on each other in times of need.

Patrick sat thinking for a few moments, then thanking the banker, he headed on over to Sheriff Hayes office to see if he had returned with any new information. Finding the Sheriff at his desk, he tried to glean more information from him about his father and was turning to go when the Sheriff said, "Son, I'm right sorry about your father, he was a good man. I don't know what I'd do if anything ever happened to my daughter. Heavens, she will be coming home from school back East later this week on the train. And once she gets settled in, I'd be obliged if you would come in to dinner some evening."

Patrick thanked the man for his sympathy, but was a little surprised about the Sheriff's dinner invitation. He had never directly mentioned his daughter to Patrick before and now Patrick couldn't remember if he had ever even known what her name was. Still, not wanting to offend the Sheriff, he agreed and said to just let him know when. As he headed over to Uncle Buck's, the local hotel, he had already forgotten about the girl and was mentally making plans to do some scouting the next morning. Maybe the killers had left some clue as to who they were or maybe where they were headed.

Mrs. Marilyn Rhodes and her daughter, Tracy, who ran Uncle Buck's greeted Patrick at the front desk. Tracy was married to a local rancher, Justin Bradley and they had three young sons. All who were quickly becoming excellent horse wranglers, just like their father. If you ever needed any horses trained, Justin was the man to see.

Whenever, Patrick had business in town, he would always stop by to say hello and eat some wonderful home cooking! Occasionally, he even played a few hands of cards with the local cowboys on Saturday night, booking a room in the hotel, since his ranch was a day and a half's ride from Brewster.

Having stayed overnight at the Hotel, Patrick rose early the next morning and headed over to the courthouse to talk with Sue Clark the County Clerk. If his father had registered the deed, the Rocking 'D' Ranch would now belong solely to Patrick, along with the new land his father had recently purchased.

Leaving the Blaine County courthouse, Patrick strode toward the livery, his mind reeling with what he had just learned. His father had not made it to the courthouse in time to register the deed before he had left town that fateful day of his death. That meant that whoever had the papers could conceivably try to claim the land.

Patrick's job now was to hunt down the killers and get back the deed to the ranch.

Saddling up the best horse the livery had to offer, Patrick headed toward his home at a steady lope, determination etched into his face.

The main ranch bordered on the northern edge of the Middle Loup River and ran up toward the North Loup River making it a large piece of prime grazing land. His grandfather, John Diamond, had started out here with just a few thousand acres, using the free range that all the ranchers used until they could file claims on the land. Eventually, he had filed, raising prime beef cattle and some of the finest horseflesh in the area. Then his son, Orville, had taken over just before the old man had succumbed to pneumonia one terrible winter.

Orville had married a young lady, Ida, from the Bilstein family over by Swan Lake, up north of Burwell. Her parents had raised eight children on their cattle ranch. The family had planted and cared for the largest private stand of trees in the whole territory, almost three hundred acres of various evergreen trees. They grew along a large spring fed lake that was the namesake of the ranch, Swan Lake.

After Orville and Ida's marriage, both had worked hard expanding their holdings of the Rocking 'D' Ranch. After several miscarriages, Ida was finally able to carry a baby to full term. A son, Patrick, was born. The couple doted on the baby, raising him with the same strong sense of pride in the land that they had worked so very hard for.

When Patrick was twelve, his mother had been thrown from her startled horse, landing in the middle of a nest of rattle snakes. She had been bitten several times and was unable to catch her horse to ride for help. When she didn't return by sundown, Orville went searching for her, finding her lying unconscious by an old cottonwood tree. Standing not far away was her saddle horse, who nickered a nervous welcome when he arrived. Orville tried desperately to revive her, but knew that too much time had passed when he saw the numerous fang marks. He cradled her in his loving arms and murmured to her as she breathed her last.

Patrick and his father had depended on each other from that day on, continuing with a deep and abiding affection not only for each other, but for the land they both loved. Needless to say, neither one was too fond of rattle snakes and killed them whenever they came across one.

Patrick arrived late that night at the Rocking 'D'. As he reined up to the barn to unsaddle his borrowed horse, his foreman, Chris Wilcoxon, met him at the barn door. They talked briefly and Chris took the livery horse on into the barn.

Chris had worked on the ranch for about ten years, and had greatly admired Patrick's father, Orville Diamond. He was a trusted friend to Patrick and would back him if he ever needed any help. Patrick knew he could be depended on to care for the borrowed animal, feed him and return him to the livery in Brewster in the next couple of days.

Patrick felt like he hadn't slept in weeks. Forcing himself to move, he went into the ranch house to his room and collapsed onto his bed, only taking time to remove his boots.

Rising early the next morning, he was determined to find his father's killers. After a hasty breakfast, he saddled up his favorite stallion, Dew Bars, and they headed north. After a few hours of riding, he found the spot where his father had been shot. Dismounting, Patrick slowly walked the area, back and forth, looking for anything the killers may have dropped.

Finding nothing at first, he almost missed the horseshoe print in some dried mud. He carefully examined it from several directions. It had a specific notch in the center of the curve. That mark identified it as belonging to his father's horse. He had always notched his horseshoes for his own horse, joking that if anyone ever stole the big red gelding, that he would be able to track down the thief.

Patrick smiled to himself, remembering his father riding the huge gelding, 'Mr. Hicks'. The horse had been almost 18 hands tall and was as cantankerous as could be to everyone but his father. They had been a great pair, he recalled, now knowing he had a prime lead to follow to locate the killers. Just for the showiness and size, Mr. Hicks, would be a horse that any man would want to own and one that no one would forget seeing. Most people just did not know his temperament. Patrick felt he could safely say there probably wouldn't be anyone riding Mr. Hicks any time soon! His father had raised the gelding and was the only person to have ever been able to stay on his back. Patrick had even tried a few times and called it a draw. The big red sorrel was definitely his father's horse and no one else's.

Mounting back on Dew Bars, Patrick headed north, catching glimpses of the special horse shoe prints from time to time. After a couple hours of riding, he arrived at the Middle Loup River. As he rode down to the edge of the riverbank, he dropped the reins of his stallion, dismounted and loosened the front cinch to give the horse a breather from the long ride. Patrick scanned the surrounding hills for any movement. He had been in the saddle since just before sunrise, taking advantage of the cool spring weather, checking on the recently branded calves and the main herd of cattle. He continued to keep eyes open for any sign of tracks and riders. It was now mid-morning and he still had a lot of ground to cover today. He figured the murdering horse thieves had kept heading north, avoiding Brewster and any ranch buildings of the neighboring ranches. It would take a rider several days of steady riding to cover just the northern section of the Rocking D, which was now one of the largest in the Sandhills Territory. It was located some three hundred miles west of the Missouri river, sharing a border with the Sioux Indian Territory, just southeast of the Black Hills. It was still a wild and free land, laced with pride and danger!

Refilling his canteen, tightening up the cinch, Patrick stopped to roll his head, trying to loosen up his muscles before remounting his stallion. He was a lean, rugged, firm muscled man, well over six foot, sandy blonde hair and piercing green eyes. He had been born and bred in this Sandhill country and loved it with all his heart and soul. He had worked and sweated over the land with his father. Now, it was his life's blood flowing through his veins and it had become as much a part of him as he was of it.

The rolling green hills, alive with wild spring flowers, covered the horizon as far as the eye could see. Cottonwoods, Cedar, and Willow trees grew in strips along the river banks, providing foliage for the area's teaming wildlife, which was plentiful. Deer, grouse, pheasants, antelope, raccoons, prairie chicken, and if a man was a halfway decent shot, he would never starve out here, Patrick knew.

That morning before he had left the Ranch, he had packed beef and deer jerky, hardtack, filled his canteen with water and tied his bedroll to the back of his saddle. He was packing a Colt 45 in his side holster, carried a Winchester rifle in his saddle scabbard and there was plenty of ammunition in the saddlebags. He was ready to ride and was hell bent on finding the men who had shot his father and stolen the deed to the ranch.

Recalling what the Sheriff had told him the previous day about his father, he knew there had been three bullet holes, all from the back. His father's pockets were empty and his gold pocket watch that his mother had given Orville on Patrick's birth was missing. His horse, Mr. Hicks, had been stolen, because it had never returned to the ranch, as loose horses will do without their rider. Patrick thought of his father and how much that pocket watch had meant to him. He swore that he would find and return it to his father, to bury it alongside the man who had loved and raised him.

Stepping into the stirrup, Patrick remounted and headed Dew Bars back toward the river, crossing at the lowest point. As the black stallion made his way across the river, the water lapped at the heels of Patrick's boots. Dew Bars lunged out of the river and up the sloping bank, heading northeast over the grass covered rolling Sandhills. Stopping at the top of the rise, both paused, when the faint sounds came to them…

CHAPTER 4

Just as they were crossing the river, upstream from the cabin, April came to with a start! She panicked and started pushing against Patrick's chest, but he tightened his hold, trying to control her flailing arms. She was yelling incoherently and struggling as Dew-Bars started to swim through the deep current of the river. Suddenly, one of her arms came free and collided with Patrick's chin, surprising him and causing his hand to slip free.

April slid into the swirling water, screaming as she went under. Patrick dove in after her, swimming in the general direction where he had last seen her. It took him several tries before finding and catching a handful of her shirt, tugging her back to him. When he turned her over to float on her back, she didn't struggle, didn't seem to be breathing. Wrapping a supporting arm around her chest, Patrick started swimming toward the closest side of the river, angling downstream, letting the current help steer him toward the shore.

The river current carried them down river and around the bend before Patrick could reach shallow water, getting his feet under him. When he gained the river bank, he lifted her limp body onto the green grass, laying her on her stomach. He started pressing on her back with firm pressure, trying to force the water from her lungs. While he worked on her, he couldn't help but feel the softness of her body, noticing her nicely rounded, but firm derriere.

Patrick sighed. He needed to quit thinking that way about her, but it was getting more difficult by the minute! I don't need to think about her, he told himself. Women are nothing but trouble! Continuing to push on her back, he forced water from her lungs and stomach. After what seemed like hours, but was only moments, she coughed, sputtered and spewed out most of the water she had swallowed in the dunking she had endured. When she had almost gained a normal breathing pattern, she sat up with Patrick's help. Then fell into his arms sobbing and mumbling incoherently. This seemed to last forever, but was only for a few minutes.

"Shhh," Patrick said, patting her on the back, "you're fine. But, you sure as heck didn't leave much water in the river, you know!"

April stopped sobbing, hiccupped tried to laugh, making only a squeaky sound. "I'm sor..

Just as she started to speak, thundering horse hooves gave them both a start. Grabbing April's arms and lifting her to her feet, Patrick glanced in the direction of a group of horsemen headed in their direction across the river.

"Come on, run!" Grasping her hand, they turned to run toward the line shack which was now only about thirty yards away further down the river bank. "We have to get to the cabin!" As they ran,

Patrick reached for his Colt. It was gone! He must have lost it in the river. But his rifle was still in the scabbard on the saddle. Patrick tried to look for Dew Bars while still running. He whistled. The stallion came running from behind the lean-to, throwing his head, sensing the danger from the approaching riders. As Dew Bars charged up alongside of the running couple, Patrick grabbed the rifle from the scabbard, pulling the canteen and saddlebags off the saddle. Then just as quickly, Dew Bars pivoted and thundered out of sight.

Turning back to April, Patrick pushed her ahead of him as they neared the cabin door. A sudden burst of gunfire splintered the wood just above the doorframe. Ducking they pushed through the door, Patrick slamming it shut just as another barrage of gunfire pocked the front of the cabin.

"W-w-what's happening?" April screamed, as she dropped to her hands and knees, scrambling into the closest corner.

"Well, I don't think they're inviting us to dinner," Patrick said as he pushed a wide plank down into place across the closed cabin door, preventing anyone from forcing their way in. "Keep your head down, while I try to see who it is!" Sliding along the front wall, then up beside the now shattered little window, he quickly glanced out, trying to locate the position of whoever was shooting at them. He could see two men down by the river behind the big cottonwood trees. Keeping low to the ground, a third was now running for the lean-to out by the horse corral.

Patrick let loose a couple shots, scattering the dust by the boot heels of the running gunman. It appeared they were all toting rifles and seemed hell bent on shooting him and the girl. But who were they? And why in hell are they shooting at us? He hadn't recognized any of the owlhoots! Bending slightly over, out of sight from the gunmen, he went to the corner where April was crouched down, trying to make herself as small a target as she could.

She was shivering cold from the near drowning in the river. Patrick grabbed a blanket from the bunk in the corner and wrapped it around her. Again, the sound of gunfire rang out, slugs hitting the outside of the cabin, plunking into the wood.

Rage was starting to build inside of Patrick. What in Sam hell was going on here? Why would anyone want to kill him or the girl for that matter. Did this have something to do with his father's killing? Someone was trying to get the ranch. Since his father was gone and the papers to the ranch were missing, if he were dead too, then the ranch would be up for grabs. There were a lot of men who would fight to take control of the Rocking D Ranch, because of the prime beef that his father and he had raised. There was a sizeable herd of good cattle horses and all the water you could ever need. The Ranch was a paradise by any man's standards!

There was another volley of gunfire. For a few minutes it became silent and still. All they could hear was the wind blowing softly through the trees, out of a now shattered front window.

Grabbing a handful of shells out of the saddlebags, Patrick reloaded his rifle. Pulling out some jerky from the packs, he took it with his canteen and handed them to the girl. "Here, eat some of this, it'll help warm you up."

April tore into the jerky like she was starved, which she was! It had been too many hours since she had last eaten. After a quick swallow, she shakily handed the canteen back to Patrick. When the first rush of hunger subsided, April was able to slow down her attack on the hapless meat. Pulling the blanket tightly around her still damp body, the shivering diminished. As she chewed on another morsel of jerky, she looked the cowboy over slowly, admiring his rugged build and the lazy blonde curl that had fallen over one eyebrow. He had lost his hat somewhere, but it didn't matter as it did nothing to detract from his appearance. Gee! He sure wasn't hard to look at and he even had a sense of humor. Yes, she was daydreaming again, but it gave her something to think about, instead of the gunmen outside!

As time crawled by, it was pierced by a few more exchanges of gunfire. When silence set in once again, April held out her hand with some jerky to Patrick, "Aren't you going to eat something?"

"I'm good for right now, but we need to get out of here, and soon," replied Patrick. The sun was beginning to set in the western horizon and it would be dark before long. They needed to keep the gunman back away from the front of the cabin, giving them time to escape. Patrick went over to the window and peered out cautiously, then fired a couple shots at the man by the lean-to, splintering the wood by the man's boot heel. The gunman quickly repositioned his foot back out of target range. Sighting with his rifle Patrick let off a shot down toward the two men who were hunkered down behind the Cottonwood trees, sending the bark flying off the tree trunks.

"What are we going to do?" April asked, "We can't go out the front door to get past them, they'll shoot us down!"

"Yeah, you're right, but we can get out another way," Patrick said, with a slight grin on his face. When he and his father had built the little cabin, they had set it back into the hill, with only the front and the two sides exposed. What no one knew, except his father, his best friend Red Feather, and he, was that there was an escape tunnel through the back wall.

April and him would have to wait until after dark to make their getaway. He knew that Dew Bars would stay close and would come to him when he whistled, but the gunmen weren't aware of that. It might give him and the girl extra time in their escape plan.

Time inched by, waiting for full dark. Sporadic gunshots were exchanged. The gunmen seemed to be firing at the cabin as if testing Patrick, to see if he still had any ammunition left. It would only be a matter of time until he did run out of shells. The plan was to be gone from here, but full dark seemed to be taking forever to arrive.

April cautiously crawled over next to Patrick, as he leaned back against the wall below the little window. She seemed to have regained some of her strength and color was returning to her cheeks. Putting her hand on his muscled forearm, she asked, "What can I do to help?" Her touch was like a branding iron, searing his skin. He didn't stop to think, he just reacted. He grabbed her to him and kissed her. Fiercely at first, then more gentle as she started to respond to him. After a few seconds of blissful forgetfulness of the situation, he drew back, gazing down into her shimmering dark eyes.

Innocently, she smiled up at him, "Did that help?"

Grinning wickedly, Patrick pulled her back for another deeper kiss. This time, he cradled her tenderly in his arms and wondered in the back of his mind, what in hell had happened to him! Had he totally lost his mind? There were gunmen outside the cabin trying to kill them and here he was kissing a girl he had just met!!! Of course, she wasn't exactly trying to stop him either! Whoa, now *that really* knocked him back!

Regretfully withdrawing his lips from her soft compliant ones, he smiled down at April. She was motionless, eyes closed, relaxed with a little smile on her face. Patrick chided her, "That's all you're getting for now".

April dreamily opened her heavy eyelids, wondering what was wrong with her! Here she was in a serious predicament, kissing a cowboy, and having funny little shivers running up and down her spine! This was just too strange, she thought. Why would she even think of letting him kiss her? He wasn't anything like her "dream man". Okay, so she *had wanted* him to kiss her. But still. He was not what she had planned for her future. That was a different kind of man. This cowboy probably was just passing through and had found her by accident. And yes, it was nice that he had rescued her, but he had also paddled her bottom, almost let her drown and then kissed her silly! Besides…

Interrupting her daydreams, April heard Patrick's voice, "get out of the cabin, but let the gunmen keep thinking we're still in here. First, we'll start a fire and make some coffee. They'll think we're settling in for the night. When it's good and dark, we'll head out."

"Leave? Are you crazy? They have us pinned down, if we try to go out that door, they'll shoot us!" She cried as she clutched at his arm.

Gently removing her hand, Patrick said, "I told you I have a way out, they'll never know we even left!"

"Sure they will, how can they not hit us?" she said, becoming frightened just thinking of what would happen if they stepped out the door into a barrage of gunfire. They would be killed and quickly!

"It'll be alright", Patrick said, patting her shoulder then rising to check out the front window again. Cautiously, he fired a shot at both parties of gunmen, while his mind sped on. He was hoping his friend, Red Feather, would be at his Tribes' Spring Hunting Ground just north of where the cabin was located. They could find refuge there with the tribe.

While he was eyeing the situation out the window, April crawled on over to the fireplace, preparing kindling to start a fire. Just as the flame caught, Patrick crouched down next to her, grabbing the old camp coffee pot off the shelf by the fireplace. Filling it part way with water from his canteen, Patrick then dumped in half a handful of coffee and sat it next to the fire.

In the next few minutes, April had a blazing fire going and pushed a standing rack over the flames. Careful not to burn herself, she lifted the coffeepot upon the rack to boil. Patrick figured the smell of fresh coffee brewing would make the gunmen think they were planning to wait out the night. This should buy him and April more time to vacate the cabin.

When the coffee came to a rolling boil, April scooted the pot to the edge of the rack. Turning toward Patrick, she raised her eyebrows in askance as to ask what was next.

"You have to be real quiet now, okay?" Patrick said very low.

"Alright," she whispered to him, following him as he crawled over to corner of the room. Patrick scooted the bunk out and away from the wall, lifting the bottom of a blanket that draped down between the bed and the wall. Hiding underneath was a small wooden door. Patrick pulled open the door not making a sound. Peering over his shoulder, April sucked in her breath, for behind it laid a hidden tunnel!

CHAPTER 5

Patrick beckoned to April to go into the dark tunnel ahead of him, "I'll be right back, just wait for me." As she crawled into the tunnel, he ran back over to the front door, removing the plank of wood that had barricaded the door. Now, if the gunmen came looking to the cabin for them, they would think they had slipped out the front without being seen. Never having any reason to thoroughly check out the interior, they would not locate the secret tunnel. Grabbing his rifle, saddlebags, canteen and a dry blanket for April, he headed into the small crawl space. Laying down the supplies, he turned back and tugged the bed back to the wall, letting the hanging blanket dropped back into place over the opening to the tunnel. Replacing the door, he felt around, locating a tin box of wooden matches. Opening the tin, he pulled out a match and flicked his thumbnail across the tip, lighting up the dark tunnel just a little. April was waiting, crouched down only a foot away, her brown eyes huge in the low light. Standing up, she whispered, "How will we be able to get out of here? That match won't last very long." In that instant the match flickered and died out.

"Just a second", Patrick whispered back, striking another match. There were several candles lying on the dirt floor, further into the tunnel. Picking up a couple, he lit them and handed one over to April.

As the light was enhanced by two candles, April was amazed at the size of the tunnel. It appeared to be large enough for even Patrick to stand fully upright without hitting his head on the ceiling. Even though it was very narrow, there was about six inches of space on either side of his shoulders. Turning back around to him, she whispered, "This is wondrous!"

With a little boy grin, he told her how he and a friend had dug this when they were younger. Patrick cautioned her as they walked, "Before we get to the end of the tunnel, we'll have to put these candles out, so the gunmen won't see any lights, just in case they have someone standing guard anywhere other than the front of the cabin."

As they cautiously emerged from the tunnel, pushing through some chokecherry trees and a few plum thicket bushes, the way opened into a thick stand of cedar trees. The trees had provided such a good cover that no one had ever found the hidden tunnel in all these years.

With only a crescent moon to see by they could just make out the outline of a neighboring hill with a dark shadow shifting back and forth. Patrick gave a soft whistle and received a muffled snort back. Silently, Dew Bars approached the two people. Patrick quickly tied the saddlebags behind the saddle and checked the front cinch. Wordlessly, he pulled his knife from a sheath in his boot and cut slits in the blanket they had brought along. Lifting it over April's head, he pulled it down over her still damp clothes. It would serve to keep her from catching pneumonia.

Mounting up, he leaned down and grabbed her arm, swinging her up behind him. As she settled in, she wrapped her arms tight around his strong back and grasped her hands together over his flat stomach, holding on as tight as she could. The recent dunk in the river was a reminder that she did not want to leave the back of the horse, if they had to cross another river.

As they eased quietly away from the stand of cedar trees, an old hoot owl called softly, causing Patrick to smile. He had recognized that "hoot owl!" After about a half mile of travel, he figured the gunmen would not be able to hear his horse running, so he urged Dew Bars into a lope. April had kept a firm grip around his midsection, tensing up, but staying completely silent. Soon, hoof beats sounded from the left of them. It was only one horse. Another "hoot" sounded thru the night. It was his friend, Red Feather.

As Dew Bars slowed his pace, April frightened, squeezed Patrick. "Why are you slowing down? What if it's one of the gunmen?" She knew she was panicking but couldn't help herself. Patrick shushed her, patting her crossed hands and drew up on the reins.

Pulling up alongside of Patrick was an Indian! April sucked in a breath to scream, but Patrick's hand squeezed her arm, reassuring her. "This is a friend of mine, he won't hurt you."

Red Feather, the son of a Sioux Indian Chief, and Patrick had been blood brothers since they were nine years old. Red Feather's tribe lived far to the northwest, on the edge of the Indian Territory in the Black Hills. A hunting party was in this area, camping at their Spring Hunting Grounds.

"What is my white brother doing, riding at night? Chasing moonbeams? Glancing sidelong at the girl, Red Feather took in her tight hold on Patrick and grinned.

Patrick ignored the question and the look, asking one of his own. "What in the devil are you doing out here? You must have lost your way home." They reached across their horses and grasped forearms, bringing to touch the scars that made them blood brothers. It had been many moons since they had last seen each other. "You always show up when there's some excitement," smiled Patrick.

Red Feather chuckled, "You mean when you need help! I was headed to your ranch when I heard gunfire. I circled back and saw you had company at the cabin! I was going to come in and help, but I see you made it out."

"Yes, thanks though. I knew that tunnel we dug would come in handy someday! We're headed up to your campground. I was hoping you would be there for the Spring Hunt. I figured we wouldn't be able to make it to Brewster or the Ranch safely, with those gunmen after us. When they figure out that we are not in the cabin, they'll start searching the area for us. I'm hoping they won't be too eager to approach until morning. That'll give us time to make it to your Tribe's Hunting Grounds."

Red Feather looked at April, whose hair was now dry and fluttering in the light breeze, "Who is your companion?"

Patrick touched April's clasped hands over his stomach and said, "This here is Sheriff Hayes's daughter, April. A couple horse thieves stole her horse and left her tied up in a thicket south of the cabin a few miles."

"What? They did not take her?" Red Feather could not believe that men would not kidnap this beautiful girl.

"Nope, she was dressed like a boy, had her hair up under a hat and was pretty scruffy looking! Then, we had an accident crossing the river, so she had a quick bath! Cleans up pretty good, I'd say", grinning as April pinched his side and smacked him in the back for his efforts!

The nerve of this man! "You just wait!" she muttered under her breathe. Dew Bars shifted nervously, reminding Patrick that they had better hit the trail before they had unwanted company, so they headed off toward the Indian encampment at a gallop. They didn't exchange any words as they traveled northward, keeping a sharp lookout for the gunmen who may or may not follow.

When the three riders arrived at the Spring Hunting Grounds, Red Feather went alone to his father's teepee and told him of the gunmen and what had happened to his friend, Patrick.

Meanwhile, Patrick and April dismounted. She looked around at the women and children now gathering around the horses. Flickering light from campfires illuminated inquisitive faces, but no one spoke. Suddenly a young Indian woman dressed in a beautiful buckskin dress, walked up to Patrick and grabbed his arm, tugging and speaking in her native tongue. As he shook his head, he gently released her hands, responding in the same language, saying something that April did not understand. Giving April a vehement glare, the Indian girl spun on her heel, stomping off behind the teepee of the Chief and out of their sight.

Looking up at Patrick, April asked, "What was she saying?"

Patrick grinned slightly and said, "Nothing important."

About that time, Red Feather came out of the teepee followed by Chief Silver Hawk, his father. The Chief greeted Patrick and April in English, asking that they set with him at the fire. Entering the large teepee they sat around the fire pit in the center and were served by the young Indian girl, who if looks could burn, April was sure she would be going up in smoke!

Patrick had warned her, quietly, before they entered the Chief's lodge not to speak, that she could be seen, but not heard, unless the Chief spoke directly to her. When they had eaten venison steak and wild greens and drank their fill of sweet spring water, Patrick told Chief Silver Hawk what had transpired. The Chief called to a young warrior standing outside of the teepee. The Chief was sending a couple warriors out to watch for the gunmen in case they had been able to follow them.

When Patrick described the men, the Chief said they had seen the tracks of three shod horses early that morning when they were hunting, but had not seen the riders.

"You will stay here until sunrise. I will give you another horse for the girl to ride", Silver Hawk said. "Red Feather will ride with you to Brewster, to make sure you arrive safely."

After a few minutes of catching up on recent news with Chief Silver Hawk and Red Feather, Patrick suggested that April needed to catch some much needed shuteye. The Chief's wife, White Dove, took April to a teepee next to their lodgings. White Dove showed the warm furs and a water gourd to April. Motioning for April to follow her, the woman took a fire torch from the outside fire and a bundle from a spot near the entry of the teepee and led April to a bubbling spring. She motioned that April could wash up here and take care of her personal needs. White Dove would return in a little while.

April was dead tired. She didn't think she had the energy to even wash, but she stripped down and sat in the small pool to soak away her aches and pains. Reaching into the bundle that White Dove had brought with them to the spring, April found a soft clean buckskin dress and a soft cloth to dry with. How thoughtful, April sighed, as she leaned back into the shallow pond.

Relaxing more as time went on her sore muscles slowly released their tension. She wondered what her father must be thinking. Of course he didn't really expect her for a few more days, so he wouldn't even know what she had done or what had happened to her until she told him when she arrived at home. Home. That was such a nice word. It had been several years since she had been home. Living at boarding school was not home. It had been lonely, but she had received letters from her father. She had made friends there, too. School had "Prepared Her For Life" as her teacher had been fond of saying. I wonder what they would think of all this, she thought.

Later, feeling like a prune, she finished her bath. She had washed her hair and began detangling it with her fingers. She did feel so much better! As she slipped the buckskin dress over her head, she couldn't believe how soft it was. It felt so comforting. Picking up the clothes she had washed out, she hung them over her arm and headed back to the teepee. As she neared the entrance, Patrick stepped out of Chief Silver Hawk's teepee.

"White Dove showed you the spring?" Patrick asked, looking at how enticing she appeared in the buckskin dress, even though her long ebony hair was still damp. Yes, she definitely was beautiful, even after all that had happened to her she was smiling. She has a strong heart, he thought. Now, where did that come from?

"Yes, she even brought me this beautiful dress, so I could wash my clothes out. They were pretty bad." She responded to his nearness and the night air seemed to hum around them. "Are we leaving in the morning? If we are, I better get to sleep". The tension caused her thoughts to ramble on. What if? Nope, that was enough of her daydreaming for today. Tomorrow was going to be a long day, she would just go to sleep and think about her future dream man. Certainly, not this cowboy! With that thought in her head, she stepped into her sleeping quarters, never seeing the yearning look on Patrick's face. *Something that even he was unaware of.*

CHAPTER 6

Even after the morning sun had risen over the horizon, April found herself still wrapped in soft furs, not wanting to move! Snuggling down further into the warmth, she recalled her dreams. They had been about her dream man. He was a tall dark stranger that danced the night away and entertained her with his charm and wit. It had been a great night for sleeping or rather dreaming!

Curling up tighter in the furs, she suddenly felt a distinct presence. Warily, she opened her eyes, when she found herself looking eye to eye with the same young Indian woman who had tried to take Patrick with her the night before. The Indian girl was glaring at her, rapidly speaking Sioux, shaking her fists, and now grabbing the fur covers from April.

April had no idea what the girl was saying to her, but if the way she was yelling was any indication, it probably wasn't good! As she started to rise up, the Indian girl shoved her back down onto the furs then jumped on top of April. She started pulling April's hair, swung an arm back to hit her and yelled what were probably curses in Sioux!

April rolled quickly to avoid the blow she knew would hurt and got tangled up in the robes. She was still trying to defend herself when the flap of the teepee flew open. Patrick and Red Feather ran in. Red Feather grabbed the girl from behind, holding her arms and tried to stop her struggling but he couldn't muzzle her voice as she continued yelling at April in her native tongue.

Patrick, grabbing April's hand, drug her from the tangled furs and pulled her flying out of the teepee entrance!

"What is wrong with her?" April demanded, as she tossed her mass of shining black hair. "I never did anything to her. I had just awakened and there she was right in my face yelling at me! Just who in the devil is she?"

Patrick laughed as he led her toward a snow white mare. "That was Little Fawn, Red Feather's sister. She thinks she is in love with me and that I should marry her".

April felt a twinge of something, and wasn't exactly sure what it was! She had only just met Patrick yesterday, but so much had happened in the last few hours that it seemed so much longer than that!

Her thoughts were interrupted when Patrick stopped in front of a beautiful white mare, "This is Snowflake. Chief Silver Hawk has given her to you."

"She is beautiful! But I can't take her as a gift!" April said stunned. "I can't, it just wouldn't be right."

Patrick laughed softly and said, "It is alright, and it's an honor for you to receive it. You really impressed the chief last night by being silent while we talked. He said he has never seen a silent white woman before!"

April laughed with him and asked, "Would you please thank him for me? She is a beautiful mare!"

"I told him that you would take good care of her and ride her with a free spirit. And from what I've seen of you so far, that, you do not lack!"

"Tell him, I am honored and I will take great care of her," April said softly, as she rubbed the mare's soft white muzzle and gazed into her deep brown eyes.

"Well, are you going to marry her?" April queried Patrick, not letting him think he could easily change the subject from the Indian girl.

But just at that moment, Red Feather came out of the teepee alone, shaking his head and grinning. He had heard April's question and knew the answer.

"Nope, she's been like that since we were kids. Besides she is my "blood sister". I couldn't marry her. Patrick stated, while watching Red Feather's face light up in mirth.

Red Feather laughed loudly, "But that never stops her from chasing him! Come, we must go before the day is past!"

April went back to the teepee and changed from the soft buckskin dress into her old jeans and shirt. Carefully, she folded the dress and went to seek out White Dove. Patrick caught up with her as she approached the Chief's teepee.

"Are you ready?" he asked, admiring the way her shrunken jeans now fit her lithe figure. And knowing she was a girl now, certainly made him look at her differently.

"Yes, I just want to thank White Dove for letting me wear the dress and her kindness." April smiled, just as White Dove appeared from the entry to the Chief's teepee.

Patrick walked over with April to White Dove and thanked her in her native tongue. White Dove responded and Patrick turned to April. "She says you are welcome, but you are to keep the dress as a gift."

"Oh," turning to Patrick and pleading, "but the dress is too beautiful and I have nothing to give her in return."

White Dove patted April's arm, saying something to her. Patrick translated, "It is a gift, she only asks that you return to visit with her."

"I would love to," April said, smiling back at White Dove, then without thinking, reached to hug the woman briefly. At first, White Dove didn't respond, then like all mothers, she returned the hug, patting April gently on the back. The two women beamed at each other before Patrick and April turned to leave.

Mounting their horses, Red Feather, Patrick and April headed southwest toward Brewster. As they left the Indian village, a few small children ran alongside calling out and waving to them. April turned back and couldn't help but smile and wave at the smiling faces of the children.

As they rode up the towering hills into the Ponderosa pines, April looked back and envied the peace and quiet of the small Indian gathering. It was so surreal here, with the river meandering along one side of the village, horses grazing contently down in the bottoms. It was simply beautiful! Too bad they had to leave so soon, she thought. It would be wonderful to stay a few days, but her father would be worried if he went to meet the train and she wasn't on it. That only gave them a few days to get to Brewster. Patrick had said it would be at least two full days of steady riding to get her home. She had almost asked him where his home was, but then thought he might not really have a home. Being a cowboy, he probably just worked for a local rancher. That's if he had a job. Since he had found her out in the middle of nowhere, and hadn't mentioned a job, he probably didn't. She kind of felt sorry for him and she didn't want to offend him, since he had saved her twice already!

Chief Silver Hawk had supplied them with food, water, and blankets when they left the village. Sleeping out under the stars, April had fallen into a deep sleep each night. They had ridden hard for the first two days, but today they were taking it slower as they were nearing the end of their journey to Brewster. When they came to the last river crossing, April said, "Patrick, I can't go home to my father like this. I'm dirty. Can't we stop, so I can wash some of this dust off?"

Patrick turned to take a good look at her and he had to laugh, because now she really did look like a scruffy lad! "Oh, I suppose we can stop, but make it quick and don't try to go swimming either," he chided her.

April dismounted eager to wash off the dust of the trail. Red Feather and Patrick rode off a little ways to keep a lookout and give her some privacy.

As April washed her face, then her hair, her mind wandered. What a coming home trip this had been! She hadn't seen her father in nearly three years. He had sent her back East to boarding school after her mother passed away. They had been living in Dodge City down in Kansas Territory, where her father was one of the Deputies. He had been offered a job as sheriff up in the Nebraska territory at a town called Brewster. The day her father had planned to leave for Brewster to take the proffered job, he had put her on an East bound train to boarding school. Over the years he had written to her about the beautiful country here in the Sandhills. He had even sent her a hand drawn map of the outlaying ranches and towns on the way to Brewster from Omaha. She had studied it diligently, daydreaming of adventure and when she would be able to rejoin her father. She had missed him terribly and now that she was a "proper" young woman, she would be able to keep house for him and have a life in a beautiful area. Maybe even marry someday! She immediately thought of Patrick. Now, that thought stopped her movements totally. Why, would he pop into her head she thought, he is nothing like what I am looking for in a future husband.

Nope. He just wouldn't do. She didn't want a cowboy or any old saddle bum! She wanted a business man, like a banker or a mayor of a town. Someone important! Someone of substance! An educated and refined gentleman, to say the least.

Like the other girls in school, she dreamed of a life of luxury. This "riding home" trip was her last thread to being "just a girl." And now that she was a woman, she would be leaving behind all her fanciful ideas and be much more mature. The girls had all talked about their futures, making big plans on marrying well, with their lives neatly planned out. Where they would live, how many children they would have. Yes, we all have our plans, she thought to herself, and mine certainly doesn't have a cowboy in it!

No, she thought as she continued washing up, she would thank Patrick kindly when he returned her to her father and never see him again! Why, he was probably just some poor broke saddle-bum, anyway. The "just passing" through kind. Yeah, that was just her luck, because he really was nice looking even though he was blonde and green-eyed.

Well, that was enough of that! She sighed, dusted off the last of the trail dirt off her clothes, mounted the little white mare and headed back to the two waiting men.

She returned looking definitely cleaner. Her hair was now braided and hanging down her back and she had a smile on her face. Patrick watched as April rode toward them. Just what was it about this girl?

He was no stranger to beautiful women. There had even been one young lady in Brewster who had caught his eye this last fall and who had made it her mission, or so it seemed, to be around whenever he was in town. Her father was the town Mayor, Roy Mueller. And her mother, Dorothy was the "society lady" for the area. The girl was a blonde-haired, blue-eyed beauty, named Carly Elizabeth. She had seemed nice enough and she had been an agreeable companion the couple of times they had met at the Church socials. Even his friend, Red Feather, had seemed entranced the one time he had met her. But he also knew that Red Feather's heart belonged to a young lady named Montana, an educated Indian girl that had been raised by an older white couple in town.

Actually, now that he thought about it, Red Feather had been quiet for the rest of that day, which was not like Red Feather at all. Knowing him as well as he did, he figured Red Feather was still trying to come up with a way to talk Montana's adoptive parents into letting him court her. He had tried but they wanted her 'to marry an educated man' as they so bluntly put it to him the last time. So he had discussed with Patrick the possibility of going back East to further his own education. Both of them had been taught by first Patrick's mother and after she died, his father made sure they learned all he had in his life, which was considerable. Jack even ordered books from back East to make sure that they knew as much about the world as was written.

Patrick's mind was drawn back to the girl in front of him. Never had he had any reactions to any woman like he had to this little spitfire, April. And that alone was certainly giving him something to think about, but now wasn't the time for such thinking he told himself. He wasn't looking for a girlfriend or anything of the kind.

Besides, April just wasn't his type. She was too darn bullheaded for her own darn good! She was more like an old porcupine! Pointy barbs, sharp as a tack! But then again, he remembered wistfully, she sure could kiss! Well, that was enough thinking like that! He would never again allow himself to be close to another woman just to be made a fool of. And he certainly didn't want anything to do with this girl, the prickly little thing!

Why, even those kisses hadn't really meant anything, it had all been in the heat of the moment! Yeah, that's right! Under these circumstances, he could see why he might be inclined to be interested in her, but he wasn't. Nope, no way! Why, he doubted they would have spoken two words to each other if they had met on the street in town.

As he came back to his senses, he saw April pulling up on the little white mare, Snowflake, directly in front of his horse. The days in the sun had darkened her already tanned skin, making freckles erupt more profusely over her upturned nose. Her curves under the old plaid shirt quickened his heart rate, causing him to shift uncomfortably in the saddle. Dew-Bars sidestepped, picking up the movement in Patrick's weight, tossing his head and nickering softly.

As the trio turned and headed southwest once again, April asked, "How much further is it to Brewster?"

"Not quite an hour," Patrick said. "Just a few more miles. As he turned to look back at her, his face drained of color. Reaching over, he slapped her mare on the rump and yelled, "Ride!"

Coming over the hill, headed their way were several riders, all riding hell bent for election! Urging their mounts into a run, Patrick pulled his rifle from the scabbard, turning to look back over his shoulder. Red Feather had likewise readied his rifle and was ready for any gunplay. Both men knew the riders coming toward them were not here for any friendly discussion.

April leaned forward, urging the mare to run faster. Glancing over at Patrick and seeing that he was watching the oncoming gunmen, she turned back around to urge the little mare to run faster and screamed! For coming straight at them from behind a grove of trees was another bunch of riders. These men had opened fire at them. Red Feather's horse went down, throwing him clear, where he now lay, unmoving. Patrick and April were forced to circle back toward the men approaching from the rear. Patrick had triggered off several shots, when suddenly he was struck by a bullet, knocking him out of the saddle.

Trying not to scream, April tried to kick Snowflake back into a run, but only made it a few yards before she was pulled from the back of the mare and tossed to the ground not far from where Patrick had fallen. She had the wind knocked out of her, but still tried to crawl toward him.

As he lay in the deep grass bleeding, Patrick pressed his hand on his left side, trying to staunch the flow of blood. It felt as if he had been jabbed with a red-hot poker in his side. He hoped that he had been lucky enough for the bullet to have passed clean through, missing any vital organs. Gritting his teeth and swearing under his breath, he tried to rise up on his elbow to see where Red Feather and April were. He prayed they both were alright. Just as he did, a rider dismounted and hit him with his rifle butt, knocking him unconscious.

Catching the sight of Patrick being struck, April was able to suck in a lungful of air. Rising to her feet, she charged the gunman, screaming her fury as she tackled him from behind. The rifle flew out of his hands, as he was knocked face first into the ground, with April sitting on top of him. Spitting out a mouthful of dirt, the man struggled to get to his feet. His first thought was that he had been attacked by a cougar! The piercing screams in his ear as April hit him repeatedly with all her might certainly re-enforced that thought. He couldn't seem to shake her off him. The crazy woman was stuck to him like a cocklebur, pummeling him with every ounce of strength she had.

Furious, April now had a hand full of the gunman's hair, pulling, while she clobbered him with the other hand. Hitting him with everything she had in her, she was kicking and hollering at him, when abruptly, she was no longer on top of him! Someone had grabbed her from behind, pulling her off the man on the ground, who now had his hands covering the back of his head.

In a semicircle, several of the gunmen sat their horses, guffawing as they watched the bundle of flying arms and legs. The one man, brave enough, who had rushed in and grabbed her, now had his hands full of a thrashing young woman. It appeared as if he was getting the worst of the battle, as he received several punishing kicks and blows from her flying feet and arms. Finally, when it looked as if the man would lose the battle, another rider dismounted and between the two men April was quickly subdued. They trussed up her hands and feet, stuffed a gag in her still screaming mouth and threw her over Snowflake's back.

It took all of a few minutes for the rage to leave April. For a few moments more she struggled while the rage subsided to just anger. She strained to see from her uncomfortable position, hanging upside down, where Patrick was. She saw his horse,

Dew-Bars, for a brief glance. He was shying away from the men, who were trying to put the unconscious form of Patrick over the saddle. Closing her eyes, she prayed that Patrick was not seriously injured. She couldn't recall where Red Feather's horse had fallen. Saying another silent prayer for him, she opened them once again. The horses were moving and she could no longer see Patrick or Dew-Bars. Fright surrounded her, and she escaped into the comfort of the swirling blackness.

Patrick slowly regained consciousness, pain bringing him back to find that his hand and feet were bound and he had a gag in his mouth. Feigning that he was not yet conscious, Patrick tried not to flinch as two men hoisted him over Dew-Bar's back, up across the saddle and tied him to the stirrups. Another rider took Dew-Bars' reins to trail the horse after his own. Patrick winched with the pain from the blow of the rifle butt, gingerly turning his head searching for signs of Red Feather and April. All he could see was the side of Red Feather's dead horse in the tall grass. He prayed that Red Feather was okay and the fall hadn't killed or severely injured him. Slowly, so not to attract any unwanted attention, he turned his head the other direction, searching for, but not finding any sight of April or Snowflake. Maybe she got away, he thought hopefully. Patrick fought to stay conscious, but was sucked back into the black void, unknowing of what had become of his friends.

CHAPTER 7

Their captors were headed northwest, when Patrick once again regained consciousness. He was feeling very woozy, but at least he was alive. Being slung over a saddle with a bullet wound would probably do that to you, he thought as he tried to take in his upside down surroundings. Trying not to attract any attention, Patrick tried to count how many men were in the party that had captured them. Close as he could tell from his inverted position, there seemed to be around a dozen men. There was a lot of arguing going on about the prisoners.

One man, who seemed to be the leader, said, "Shut-up and ride. We need to clear outa here now, we're too damn close to town!"

After about an hour or so of steady riding, they came to what looked like an abandoned homestead by a large beaver dam. While most of the gang dismounted and unsaddled their horses, some of the men untied the prisoners from the horses and carried them into an old shed. Removing the gags, they gave them a small drink of water. Having regained consciousness only minutes before they arrived, April was glad to be free of the dirty gag and greedily swallowed the water. Tipping her head up, April looked at the man and pleaded, "Why did you take us? What is it you want?" He grunted and scowled back at her. Then, like a bolt out of the blue, it dawned on her! She recognized him! He was one of the men who had stolen her horse in the first place!

"Why you no account horse thief! You're one of the men who stole my horse! You left me there to die! You're gonna pay for this!" She yelled, kicking at him with her bound feet. Catching him in one shin, he yelled, shoving her backwards into some moldy old hay next to Patrick who lay silently next to her as the bandits locked them both in the shed. From the sounds outside the door, the men had braced an old log or something heavy up against the door. Silence followed for a few seconds, but only until April started to yell some more at the men. Patrick quickly nudged her in the side with his elbow and shook his head.

Whispering he said, "I'm glad that you're okay! But you have to be quiet!"

Looking back at the door, April started to raise her voice to rant again, "But, he's one of the men who stole my horse."

He shushed her and spoke quietly, "Listen, the more ruckus you make, the more liable they are to do something to shut you up! So please be quiet! I need to think, did you see where Red Feather was? I seen his horse go down, but that's all I remember."

April just shook her head no, feeling the reprimand and not sure what to say as she knew she had been very selfish. She had forgotten that Red Feather's horse had fallen and she didn't know what happened to his rider.

After a few minutes, which seemed like hours to April, Patrick said, "First, we need to get loose. Turn your back to me and let me see if I can get the ropes off your hands". Patrick used his teeth to pull on the ropes binding April's wrists behind her back. The bleeding from his wound had slowed to just an oozing trickle of blood, but his shirt and pant leg were thoroughly soaked. The blood was starting to dry, stiffening the material.

His side burned like wildfire, but he knew they didn't have much time. As he pulled on the ropes, he felt one strand loosing, "There, try to pull your right hand out," he whispered.

April tugged her hand till it came free and pulled the remaining rope off her left hand. Quickly, she untied her feet and then untied Patrick's hands. Pulling himself upright into a sitting position, he pulled the binding rope from his feet. April tried to get a look at his wounded side, there was so much blood, she thought. "Are you alright?" She whispered, as she reached to touch his side.

He flinched, sucked in a deep breath, whispering hoarsely back, "it hurts like hell, but it won't stop me from moving! Now try and see if you can spot anyone out of the cracks on the front of the shed. But, be very careful, don't let them see or hear you! We don't want them to get suspicious. I'll check the back and sides!"

They both silently circled the interior of the shed, checking for the men and looking for a possible way out at the same time. In a few moments, they met by the back wall of the shed. Sitting there was an old chest, some harnesses, and farm tools scattered about in the old hay. They had apparently been left behind when the previous owners had vacated the homestead.

As she approached the rear of the shed, she walked up to Patrick, looking up at him, tears rolling down her cheeks, "I'm so sorry, we keep getting into all these messes and I don't know why! What did I do? I feel like I'm in a bad dream!"

Patrick leaned down and put his arm around her, giving her a careful hug, favoring his bad side, "It's okay, I'll get us out of this."

He needed to sit down and take a breather. His side was on fire and he was starting to feel a little lightheaded. The dusty old wooden chest sat close to the back wall of the shed. Maybe, if he could sit there and catch his breath, he could think better. As he started to place his weight on the corner of the chest, it gave way, almost dumping him onto the floor. It slid backward, exposing an opening in the floor, barely visible in the dim light.

"Hey," he whispered, "look at this! It must be a cover for a root cellar or something".

Reaching out her arm and touching him on the shoulder to steady herself, April stepped carefully over to the side of the chest. With only the waning light from sunset filtering through the walls of the shed, she peered down into the dimness of the opening. She thought she could see a ladder that led down into some kind of room. "What are we waiting for?" she whispered back and started climbing down the narrow ladder. Patrick followed her, fishing out a match from his one dry pants pocket and striking it on the wooden step. The light flared, briefly, showing some wooden shelving with some old canning jars, some empty and some filled with food that had been left behind. Within arm's reach was an old lantern, grabbing it, Patrick quickly lifted the glass globe, catching the wick on fire. Slowly, he turned it down, regulating the burning wick and dropped the globe back into its brackets. There didn't appear to be much oil in it, but he hoped it would last as long as they needed it, however long that might be. As he looked around, April grabbed his arm and whispered, "Look! Over there!"

In one corner, there appeared to be an old door, hap-hazardly built, but still looking every bit like a door. Grasping the old leather handle, Patrick pulled it toward him. He tugged gently at first, then harder as it refused to budge. Then without warning it fell toward him. Catching the door in time to keep it from crashing to the floor and making any noise, he laid it against the side of the small area, up against the shelves.

"Wait here and let me check this out." he told April. Then stepping over a small pile of old discarded rags, he picked up the old lantern and went through the small entrance leaving April waiting in the root cellar. Rubbing her arms in the draft that came from the opening, she tried to remain quiet and patient. But as patience had never been one of her virtues, she started toward the opening, calling softly to Patrick.

"Patrick?" "Patrick…" Maybe, I should just try to follow him. Just a little further… I can see the light once I get through that doorway, she thought. She suddenly did not like the feeling of being here all alone. Before she could make up her mind about actually going through the doorway, Patrick's arm with the old lantern reappeared.

"What's in there?" she asked, thankful for both him and the light.

"Just hold on a bit, okay?" Patrick said as he handed the lantern to her. Climbing up a step on the ladder, he reached up to pull the chest back over the opening. He hoped the gunmen wouldn't notice any slide marks in the hay.

Retrieving the lantern from April he motioned for her to follow him back through the small doorway. It led them into a narrow tunnel for a few feet, looking like it had been crudely chiseled out of the surrounding limestone. Further on, they could see that it became a natural tunnel. Holding the lamp, Patrick continued onward with April following close behind him, slipping ever deeper into the dark recesses. After a few minutes, Patrick noticed the elevation of the path went down sharply, curved for a few yards then leveled out. When they rounded another curve they found themselves in a small cave. It had a low ceiling with what appeared to be little shelves chiseled out of the rock wall. It had been furnished with a couple of old wooden crates, a small stand, and a dusty old cot with a rotting old blanket lying on top. Someone had used this area as a living space for hiding from Indians or taking shelter from possible tornadoes which were common here in the hills.

"My father never said anything about there being any caves in the Sandhills", April whispered quietly. She was extremely awed that something like this was here in this country. She wondered if anyone else had ever known about caves in this area. Everyone she had known in the Kansas Territory, knew that the country there was littered with caves of all sizes. She could hardly wait to tell her father about this new discovery!

Patrick answered, "I've heard there were some, but you never believe it till you see it! I imagine that most people never know about them. Come on, we need to move on. No telling how long before that bunch comes back to the shed to talk to us!"

They continued following the tunnel which led them away from the small cave, walking as quickly as they could. Soon they encountered another very small cave, but it had three tunnels leading somewhere. Patrick started with the first path on the left, hitting a dead end, so they returned and took the next tunnel. It had been another dead end. Coming back to the little cave, they both knew there was only one path left to take. Reaching for April's hand, Patrick now headed down the last tunnel, praying it would finally lead them away from the old homestead and not just another dead end with no escape.

Each trip down one of the tunnels had used a lot of time, back tracking, and then heading off in a new direction. As he searched, Patrick hoped the gang had not caught Dew Bars as he had bolted from the men when Patrick was taken off his back. If the horse was loose, they might have a chance to escape. Providing they could find a way out of this cave menagerie! He was worried about his friend, Red Feather. He knew that Red Feather's horse had been shot down out from under him, but didn't know just how bad Red Feather might be hurt or if any of the gunmen had gone back to make sure he was dead.

Continuing through the tunnel, Patrick tried to remember exactly what has happened. He didn't recall seeing anyone pay any attention to Red Feather or the dead horse. The gunmen only seemed to be interested in him and April. Which, brought up another question. Why? None of this deal made any sense. Why had they not killed him immediately this time? It seemed they had been definitely trying at the line cabin! There had to be more to what was going on then he could see right now. But first, they had to get out of here, then go back to check on Red Feather.

Halting suddenly, Patrick whispered, "Hold it! Did you hear something?

April ran into the back of him with an oomph of air escaping her lungs. She tried to listen, but her heart was pounding too loudly in her straining ears.

She was aware only of clutching Patrick's hand with one of her own.

"There it is again". Holding his breath, he listened in the low illumination of the old lamp, he unconsciously gripped April's hand tighter.

April turned slightly, then shook her head and started to speak….I..

"Shh", he whispered, shaking his head and waiting.

Once again, the sound drifted to him, only slightly louder this time. It was an owl hooting. It couldn't be! Red Feather? But it had to be him, for no one but him and Red Feather ever used that call to each other. How in heavens name did he get here? His horse had been shot and they had surely traveled several miles from the place where they had been attacked!

Patrick tugged on April's hand, pulling her forward on through the tunnel, noticing that the path now seemed to rise slightly uphill in elevation. Again, they heard the owl hooting call, but it was much louder now. Patrick sent one answering call. Upon turning a corner they came upon the "owl". Red Feather was standing in the center of a large cavern, the size of a barn. He hurried over to them and stopped within the circle of light from their lantern.

Not believing what she was seeing, April gasped, "Red Feather, are you alright?"

Patrick clasped Red Feather's shoulder, "I am really glad to see you're alive, but how did you get here so quickly? It has to be several miles from where we were attacked."

"I figured they thought I had been killed in the fall when they shot my horse, so I just played dead until they left. I tracked them for a couple miles when.."

Before Red Feather could finish, there was a noise and from behind him stepped his sister, Little Fawn!

"W-w-what are you doing here," April sputtered.

"I've come to rescue the man I love!", Little Fawn stated defiantly while grasping Patrick's arm and pulling him away from April. Reacting without a thought, April bristled and grabbed Patrick's other arm, not yet realizing that Little Fawn was speaking English!

"Okay, that's enough for now", Patrick said, freeing his arms from the two women and stepping in between them.

Red Feather took Little Fawn's arm, tugging none too lightly, "We need to get out of here, now. I'll tell you everything later, we have to leave pronto!"

"Yes", Patrick said, looking at his friend, "we need to hurry! If some of those gunmen get their way, I don't think they will wait too long before coming to get us from the shed. They were arguing over what they were going to do on the ride here."

Single file, the four of them left the large cavern and went down the exiting tunnel. The air became moist and cool. They could now hear a distant roaring sound.

"What is that noise?" April asked as they drew closer to the sound.

"It's a waterfall", Red Feather said. As they traveled another twenty feet, they suddenly came to a sharp turn which opened into a large cavity. Green iridescent moisture covered the floor and walls of the cave. It glistened in the reflected light from the lantern just behind a roaring water fall. The area was filled with a roiling mist, partially concealing Dew Bars, Snowflake and Little Fawn's horse. The mounts shifted about nervously, wide-eyed and waiting. Dew Bars nickered softly, tossing his glossy main, as if to say, "hurry up"!

At the front area of the cave was a cascading wall of water, about four feet wide and eight feet tall. The water was flowing over a rock ledge then dropping down just a few inches into the river bed.

Amazed, Patrick turned to Red Feather, "I never knew this was here, how did you?"

Red Feather grinned, "I never tell all my secrets to you, even if you are my blood brother! Come, let's go, it is already dark."

"Good, that should give us some cover," Patrick said. "If they don't intend to come for us until tomorrow at daybreak, that should give us enough time to get to Brewster! But, let's not leave anything to luck, okay? Let's head out!"

Carefully, they led the horses out through the waterfall and mounted up. April rode double with Patrick, they took the lead. Little Fawn followed and Red Feather brought up the rear. Threading their way through the tall pine trees, the riders were close to the bottom of what appeared to be a large valley. The sun had already dropped out of sight, throwing the last rays of subdued golden light on the tops of the pines. Birds called to each other as the riders invaded their territory, flushing out from the trees as they passed through. After a half hour of walking their horses to lessen the sounds of their leaving the area, they were finally able to nudge them to a faster pace, angling downhill and back toward the southeast and Brewster. Upon reaching the grassy meadows, the horses were released into a ground eating gallop. At this pace, Patrick figured they should reach Brewster in a couple hours. As they rode swiftly across the valley, the men repeatedly scanned their surroundings, checking to see if they had been followed. The girls did their part by watching ahead for any signs of unwanted company.

The moon was just rising in the east as they topped the last range of hills north of Brewster. The town's flickering lights beckoned them, welcoming them home. It had been a hard punishing ride. The horses were spent and the riders exhausted from the last few hours of intrepid events. Patrick's wound was hot and burning to the touch. It would need to be cleaned out to prevent any infection from setting in. Otherwise, he thought, he might be saving someone the trouble of killing him. Ha! But, that thought sobered him up, making him ponder on what in Sam Hill was going on?

As they dismounted at the livery barn, the hostler, Edward Akin, came to take the reins of the horses. He was an Scotch Irishman, who had started the livery when Patrick had been a young lad. "Give them some grain and a good rubdown, they deserve it," Patrick said, handing two silver dollars to the man.

"Aye, sir." The hostler nodded his head at Patrick and continued, "The sheriff, he just got back in ta' town from the Guggenmos Ranch, about an hour 'go. He said he was wantin' to speak with ya, sir, if'n I was to see you. Seems like they had some trouble down there in the last few days."

"What happened?" Patrick questioned him, as he held his hand over his side. He wasn't feeling so good all of a sudden. Things seemed to be moving around him. The lantern light was fading in and out of focus and his hearing seemed to be growing dimmer.

"Now, ya know sir, he didn't rightly say. Just that they had some troubles. He said, if I was ta' see ya' though, to tell ya to come to him soon."

"Okay, thanks Edward, I'll do that." As Patrick turned to go out of the livery door, he thought things were awful dark for it being a full moon. Then, it dawned on him that it wasn't the dark of night. As he collapsed against the doorframe, the last thing he heard was April's scream.

CHAPTER 8

Before Patrick's body could hit the ground, Red Feather caught his friend. Lifting him easily, he asked Edward to take them to the Doctor. April's face was white as snow, she walked to one side of Red Feather and Little Dawn walked on the other as he followed Edward.

An unspoken prayer was running through April's mind. She was afraid of something happening to the cowboy who had once again protected her. She couldn't explain why she was feeling this way. It was just gratitude she told herself once again, that's all. Unconsciously, she reached out for Little Fawn's hand giving a slight squeeze. Both of them were looking at each other with the same thought that Patrick would be alright. It seemed to bring peace between them, at least for the time being.

Edward pounded on the Doctor's door calling out, "Hey Doc, we got a wounded man that needs your help!"

Within seconds the door opened and they were ushered in by Doctor Thomas L. Therien. "Put him up there on the table Red Feather and get his shirt off. Edward take and get these girls out of here 'cause it won't be pretty to watch! I'll holler if we need any help, but I think Red Feather can hold him if need be."

Going out the door, both girls looked back at the limp form lying on the doctor's table, the blood stained clothes and the very pale face of the man they both cared about, although one of them would not admit it even to herself.

Doc Therien arranged a tray of instruments and set it next to the wounded man. Poring some alcohol over his hands then shaking off the excess he picked up a swab of gauze and proceeded to clean around the small but ghastly wound. Inspecting it and probing to make sure there was not a bullet still lodged in it, he then motioned to Red Feather. "Roll him onto his stomach so I can clean the exit wound. This boy was mighty lucky it passed all the way through and missed his organs. Looks like he has lost a lot of blood, but otherwise he should come through this ordeal just fine."

Red Feather was relieved to hear such encouraging news from the Doctor. Watching and helping the doctor bind up the wound, he felt compelled to ask, "did you always know you wanted to be a doctor?"

Doc stopped and looked up at the tall Indian thoughtfully. "Not really, I was about your age when cholera took both of my parents. I felt helpless not knowing what to do for them. It helped me make a decision that I will never regret. I went to school here in the States and even went over to England for a few years to learn all that I could about medicine.

Now, here I am a Doctor and there is nothing like the reward of making someone feel better or to save a life."

Red Feather listened, then asked, "Do you think I would be able to go to the White Man's medical school?"

"If you are dead serious about this Red Feather, I will help you and make sure that you are able to go to medical school. I would be honored to do that. Let's finish up here, get Patrick into the bed in the spare room and then we'll sit down and talk about it."

"Thank you", Red Feather stated knowing he was making a firm committment to his future and in establishing the pathway to winning Montana's parents approval.

Settling Patrick into the bed, Doc Therien sighed, when he looked up at Red Feather, "we'll let him rest now and I'll check on him periodically. I figure by now everyone is wondering how Patrick's doing, so let's go let them know."

At sometime during the night, Patrick was pretty sure he could hear voices, but he couldn't quite make out what they were saying. They seemed muffled, sounding far away. As he lapsed back into unconsciousness, Doc Therien had been busy telling Sheriff Hayes, Little Fawn and April how his patient was doing and what the problem was.

Doc Therien explained that he had checked the wound for a bullet and not finding any had proceeded to clean and suture the gunshot wound. It appeared that it had been a straight through shot. The bullet had caused extensive bleeding but not a lot of damage to Patrick's side. He explained to the worried group that Patrick had collapsed from the lack of blood but would be alright in a few days. Right now he needed bed rest and food to help him regain his strength. With proper care and rest the wound would heal up in a few weeks.

April's father, Sheriff Hayes, said they'd check on Patrick in the morning, as he led April out of the doctor's office. Once outside, he stopped to talk with Red Feather and Little Fawn. "Do you have a place to sleep tonight," he asked.

"We will camp south of town," Red Feather stated, "and come in to check on Patrick in the morning."

Placing a hand on Red Feather's shoulder, Sheriff Hayes said, "I wouldn't hear of it! I have enough room for both of you, so come with me. I'll fix you something to eat and then we can all get some rest. It's the least I can do for you saving my girl!"

Nodding acceptance, Red Feather and Little Fawn followed the sheriff and April back to their house. Sheriff rounded up some cold roast beef and biscuits, serving it with some hot coffee. When they had all finished eating, Little Fawn and April, without speaking to each other, cleared the table. Sheriff Hayes showed the brother and sister to bedrooms across the hall from each other, thanking them again for bringing his daughter home safely. Little Fawn started to snort her feelings, but Red Feather gently pushed her into her room, thanking the Sheriff for the meal and bed. Then, he too turned into his bedroom and shut the door.

As father and daughter walked down the hall, Sheriff Hayes shook his head, "Lordy, girl, you could have given me a heart attack! What in the world did you think you were doing, riding home alone all those miles? You don't know how lucky you are to be alive! You're quite fortunate to have had someone like Patrick find you! What those other men could have done to you, God only knows! Your mother would turn over in her grave if she knew!"

Looking up into her father's stern face, she pleaded, "Father, please don't be mad! I know I got a lot of people in trouble, but I needed to be alone! I'm not your little girl anymore. I'm all grown up!"

"You call what you did, grownup? Why, I ought to turn you over my knee and wallop the living daylights out of you! You could have been killed or worse!" But his anger dwindled as he stopped in front of her room and saw the tears well up in her eyes.

"Well", April sighed, "you won't have to. Patrick already did!" She explained part of what had taken place when Patrick had first found her.

"I knew there was something I liked about that young man!" Sheriff Hayes said, laughing quietly. "But, you still have to answer to me!

Tomorrow, we are going to sit down and discuss this whole mess! Go on to bed and get some rest. He gave her a hug, kissed her cheek and patted her back, then turned to go.

Suddenly, reaching out and touching his arm, April said quietly, "Father, I've missed you so much!"

Sheriff Hayes turned back and smiled, giving her another squeeze and a kiss on her forehead, "And I missed you, too! I really am glad that you are home safe and sound. But don't you ever even think about doing something foolish like that again! Understand?"

"Yes, father," April said through the tears running down her face. Never, had she been so happy to once again be "daddy's" little girl.

CHAPTER 9

Early the next morning, the smell of brewing coffee woke Patrick up. Awww, but he was awful stiff and sore. As he ran his hand across the bandages on his side, Patrick wondered how long he had been out of it this time.

Just then, Doc Therien entered the room, "Hey there, young man, glad you're awake. You up for a cup of coffee?"

"Sure," Patrick said, painfully raising himself up on his elbow, "soon as I get dressed."

"Whoa there…young man, you're not going anywhere! You need to rest and get your strength back, son. You have lost a lot of blood. Maybe in a couple days, I'll let you get up and walk around, but not today!" The Doctor placed a cup of black steaming coffee on the nightstand next to Patrick's bed. I expect the sheriff will be here shortly. He'll want to know what all has happened. Hey, isn't that daughter of his a surprise? I thought she was to arrive on the train this week."

Patrick remained silent, gingerly picking up the proffered hot coffee off the nightstand. Taking a cautious sip, he gazed over his cup of coffee to the doctor. "Yeah, you could say she's something, alright!" He was silently remembering all that had transpired between him and the wild little demon! Ha! Taking another swallow of the coffee, he couldn't hold back giving some of his opinion, "She sure seems to be mighty independent on making her own travel plans, anyway". Settling himself back into his pillows, enjoying the hot coffee, he pondered what she might be doing this morning. Had she told her father anything yet? But ,as fate would have it, just as his memory was drifting back to when he had first kissed her, the door opened and in walked her father, Sheriff Hayes and Red Feather.

"Good morning, Sheriff, Red Feather." Doc said, "would either of you gentlemen like a hot cup of coffee?"

"Not right now," Sheriff Hayes stated, as he drug up a chair next to Patrick's bed. "First, I need to hear the whole bag of details on what's been going on with my daughter and how you got shot!"

"Yes, sir," Patrick answered, sitting the coffee cup back over onto the nightstand. He reached down to straighten his blankets, gathering his thoughts, before looking back at the slightly scowling Sheriff.

"Let's just start with my daughter, why don't we?" Sheriff Hayes said as he leaned slightly forward, looking directly into Patrick's eyes.

Silence permeated the air. No one moved or spoke. Not even Doc Therien. Shifting back into the chair, the Sheriff turned looking up at first Red Feather then back to Patrick.

"Okay," he drawled, "just jump right in either one of you and tell me what in hell has been going on? I want some answers and I want them now!" The Sheriff slammed his fist onto the nightstand causing the hot coffee to slop over the rim.

Patrick glanced up from his prone position at Red Feather, who lifted one eyebrow and held his open palm toward him. Effectually telling Patrick to jump right in, as the Sheriff had so kindly put it.

"Okay, a couple days ago, I ran across her. April that is. She was hogtied in some brush on the northern section of the ranch," Patrick started. Sometime later, he finished with their arrival at Brewster the night before. Conveniently leaving out the part about spanking her and especially the kissing part, unaware that the Sheriff already knew about the spanking part.

Sheriff Hayes rose from his chair, "From some of the descriptions, it sounds like the men who robbed the bank. They are most likely tied in with the killing of your father and stealing the ranch deed. Did you overhear any one of them talking about a bank robbery? Or, did any of you get a good look at these men?"

Patrick shook his head, "I've never seen any of them before. Except one did look a lot like Doc Middleton, but I know Doc's face and it wasn't him. Do you know if he has a brother or close relative in this area?"

"I'll check into it," Sheriff Hayes said, as he rose and walked toward the door. "Anything else, you might have overheard? Think real hard."

"Nothing," Patrick replied, "just them arguing about whether or not they should kill us. But, I can take you back there to the place they were holing up in. I'll be ready at sunrise tomorrow. Red Feather, I think you will want to take Little Fawn back home to the Tribe, they are probably worried sick about her missing."

Red Feather laughed, "You do not know her very well, these days. She comes and goes as she pleases. But this time I will have help in taking her back, for it seems Lone Wolf has shown up for her. He has been wooing her for months now. She tries to say she is in love with you, but I see her eyes following him every time he visits the camp. She protests too much our mother says. I do believe his coming all the way here for her will be a deciding factor. Lone Wolf has much to offer her as Chief of the River Tribe. He cares for her and I think she is just now realizing her own feelings. I saw how she reacted when he came to the Sheriff's house this morning."

Patrick smiled at Red Feather, "I've met Lone Wolf, he is a good man and he will certainly have his hands full with Little Fawn!"

Both of the men laughed, knowing Little Fawn's perchance for orneriness. She would probably lead Lone Wolf on a merry chase but would capture him when she was ready. It was a good feeling to know that his childhood friends were happy.

Red Feather gathered up his rifle by the door, "I must go and help with the spring hunt! I will see you again, so do not get yourself into trouble, while I am gone!" They clasped forearms in farewell and Red Feather left the room.

A few minutes and a couple more questions later, the Sheriff and Doc Therien left the room, finally leaving Patrick alone. Pulling himself up to a sitting position, he started looking around the room for his clothes. Not seeing them in plain sight, he thought they might be in the armoire over in the corner. Gritting his teeth and sucking in a breath, he carefully but somewhat painfully swung his legs out of the covers and over the edge of the bed. Just then, April walked thru the door.

"Oh my", she blushed, covering her mouth with her hand, but still looking intently at Patrick sitting on the edge of the bed with a sheet only half covering his manly parts. For what seemed a lifetime she couldn't move or speak.

Patrick was so shocked to be caught half naked, he didn't move for a second or so, but just stared back at her. Coming back to himself, he quickly covered himself with the rest of the sheet, his face flushed and scowling. What in heaven's name was she doing here now? He thought. This wasn't exactly where he thought he wanted to be alone with her. Not with her father just outside!

Now where in hell did that thought come from? *Alone with her?* He didn't even want to be "around" her, she was nothing but trouble! Ignoring his mind, his body had responded to her presence and stare. Grabbing the other blankets he covered up and lay back down. He knew his face was red, for it felt like it was on fire. What in the world was happening to him? His body was reacting to her like a stud with a mare. He didn't know if he was losing his mind or what! Even without looking at her, he could envision her long dark hair spread out on a blanket of grass, with him over her, making love to her. Kissing her and caressing her to heights that he was sure she'd never been to before. Making her totally his. Damn! That did it! He was getting out of here and away from her as soon as he could ride!

Watching the emotions wash over Patrick's face, April was wondering what he was thinking about! Heavens to Betsy! With the thought of what she was thinking about, that could only mean one thing! With her face starting to flame up, April turned and ran, passing her father in the hallway, stammering that she would see him at home.

Sheriff Hayes, shaking his head, looked after her, wondering what in the devil had happened now! Young people! They could drive a man to drinking, trying to figure out what they were doing and thinking! Turning around and going back down the hall, he walked back into the bedroom. Looking Patrick over slowly, he took notice of his heightened color and asked, "Want to tell me what just set my girl on fire?"

Patrick scowled back at him, "Hell, if I know!"

Exasperated, Sheriff Hayes turned and walked out of the room and into the hall, when suddenly it hit him. He had to chuckle. Well now, maybe April had finally met her match and she just didn't know it yet!

Meanwhile, April walked silently back toward home, her emotions running up and down a very steep pathway. What, had she been thinking of? She had no idea what had caused the kinds of thoughts she had when seeing Patrick in such a state of undress. She must be losing her mind. She just needed to calm down, that was all. I will just forget about him, he is not in my future. I know what I want! And it certainly is NOT HIM!

But Patrick continued to invade her thoughts as she daydreamed her way home. Walking on, she was completely missing the beautiful and quiet scenery of the town. Trees shaded her path where she stepped, flowers popping up in the flower boxes at the windows of the houses she walked by.

That man! He set her heart to pounding, just looking at him. Why couldn't he have been someone well to do, someone important, like a banker or the mayor. She wanted a man of financial means, who could provide for her, a man who she could stand beside and share his position in the community. Or as her Dad said, not someone who didn't have a pot to pee in or a window to throw it out of!

For Heaven's sake, he didn't appear to have any money. Let alone a job. Patrick didn't even seem to be concerned about making a living or just where his next meal was coming from. He was just a saddle tramp. It was really very sad, when she thought about it. He was really kind of nice looking, in a rugged way....okay, admit it to yourself, dummy, she thought, sighing wistfully. He was Great Looking! And ooh Lordy, could he kiss! He would be a real catch, if only...

Well! She decided she wouldn't keep thinking of HIM! That just wouldn't do! She would just have to find that someone else. One who could meet all her expectations!

As she meandered down the street, she started making mental plans. First, she would meet the other women of the community. Why, there might even be a Sunday Social at Church this week. All the important people, including the single ones, went to the Church Socials. She could possibly meet someone there.

She would have to ask her father when he returned, for he surely knew about those things. As she turned the corner by the Church, a man was crossing the street smiling and seemed intent on talking to her. As he approached, she smiled brightly, thinking to herself. Now here I am, with an opportunity to meet new people and make new friends! As the man drew within a couple feet from her, his smile disappeared. Grabbing her arm and wrenching it behind her, he quickly put his hand over April's mouth and pushed her into the heavily wooded area behind the church.

Stunned at first, April was motionless, then was forced to moan in pain as the man twisted her arm harder and shoved her deeper into the woods. Every time she struggled, the man would put more pressure on her twisted arm, increasing the hurt of her already throbbing shoulder. After a few minutes of being forced to walk along an old pathway, April noticed a horse tied to an old broken down wagon. The wagon must have been there for years as the grass and small saplings were growing up through the bed and two of the wheels that were now leaning off-center of the axle.

When they approached the horse, the man removed his hand from her mouth. April had been waiting for just such an opportunity. She screamed at the top of her lungs, turning and shoving the man backwards over one of the old broken wagon wheels. Grabbing her skirts, she lifted them and ran as fast as the overgrown old narrow path would allow! She continued to scream, hoping and praying that her father was on his way home and could possibly hear her. Then, just as she was about to gain her freedom from the grove of trees, she was grabbed from behind, spun around and hit with a clenched fist! She dropped like a ton of bricks!

The man, an outlaw of little notoriety, now stood over her. He was breathing hard and muttering about what a pain in the neck this girl was turning out to be! The boss should have just let him kill her and that cowboy when they had the chance, he thought. That would have stopped all this nonsense of chasing them around the blasted country! It was all getting to be mighty irritating! After catching his breath, the man pulled April up and threw her limp body over his shoulder. Heading back to his horse, he decided this was the last time he was going to do this kind of job! Robbing a train or a bank was one thing! But, this chasing people around, having them escape repeatedly and then chasing them some more was just not his cup of tea! He was having serious doubts about having gotten involved with this mess in the first place. Never again! He would deliver her to the boss and then he was hitting the trail. He had had enough!

Arriving back at his tethered horse, he threw the still unconscious April, none too gently, over the front of the saddle, then mounted up and headed deeper into the grove of trees. The Boss better be happy, he thought, because this was the last time he was going chasing after some skirt! She probably didn't know anything about the danged gold anyway!

CHAPTER 10

Ooh! April moaned, touching her jaw gingerly with one hand. What had that man hit her with, an anvil? She slowly forced her eyes open to soft muted golden sunlight reflecting on the ceiling of a small bedroom. April stayed lying on her back, trying to focus her eyes. Slowly looking around the room, she noted that the door was closed and the window was boarded up from the inside, which seemed strange. Didn't you normally board up a broken window from the outside? Only a few streaks of sunshine were able to find their way through the old weather beaten boards, making the room seem smaller than it really was, and at this moment it sure felt like a prison cell.

Well, at least she wasn't trussed up with ropes and a gag in her mouth, she thought. Gingerly, she pulled herself upright while holding onto the side of the narrow bed, sliding her feet down to the hardwood floor.

Gazing around the room, she silently prayed. God, help me! I shouldn't be so dad-blasted trusting! I should have waited for my father to walk me home. If, I just hadn't gotten flustered at Patrick! I could have been walking home with my father and I sure wouldn't be in this place! Lord! The messes I get into! Nope, I can't panic, I won't panic! I've gotten out of the other messes just fine! I can do this, I just have to think rationally, that's all!

First, though, why would they kidnap me? I don't have any money and neither does my father. So, it can't be for a ransom. At this time, April didn't know the story of Patrick's father's shooting or anything else for that matter.

Just as she stood up, the door banged open against the wall and a middle aged man walked in, carrying a tray of food and a water pitcher. Setting it on a small trunk by the boarded up window, he cast a glance in her direction and said, "Here's some grub. You had better eat something. You've been out of it since they brought you here and you may be here awhile, yet." Turning to leave, he looked at her again, shaking his head sadly.

Stepping in his direction, April pleaded with him to wait, "Please, why am I here? What do you want with me?" But, the old man continued on his way out.

Quickly, she tried to follow him to the door in hopes that she might slip past him and get away but as she neared the door an armed man stood just outside watching and frowning dourly at her. The older man kept going and the gunman slammed the door in her face. She heard a key click, locking her in the room.

Well, pleading didn't work. From what the old man had said, she had been knocked out cold for several hours. She figured it was the next day after her abduction. Still feeling a little woozy, she turned back slowly to the bed. Just to rest a bit, she told herself, but when she laid down she fell into a dreamless sleep. The day passed without awareness of the fleeting time.

When she awoke the next day, her first thought was on how to find a way out of here. Looking around the room again, she let her gaze pause at the window. A little weak, she decided to have a look at that window! Walking over to the boarded up window, she tried to fit her fingers in some of the small cracks in the boards covering the window but there wasn't enough room. Then, she realized that there wasn't any glass in the window. That would mean that this was an old abandoned house and no one lived here. So there wouldn't be any help coming from that quarter either.

Not knowing what else she could do about escaping right this minute, she went over to the narrow bed and sat down. This whole mess was getting stranger all the time. She had lost a whole day and night and most of this day already and she figured maybe the old man had been right. She really ought to eat something, to keep her strength up.

Even though the food from the previous night was cold, she ate. And once she started eating, she realized just how hungry she was. Cleaning the plate and drinking enough water to refresh herself, April then tore a piece of material from her petticoat, dampened it with some of the water and laid it on her face as she reclined on the small bed. I'll just rest a little bit and think of a way out of here, she thought, as she dropped into another deep exhausted sleep.

Voices rising and falling in anger cause April to awaken from her much needed rest. It sounded like there were several men disagreeing over something! She rose to her feet and went quietly to the door. She tried the door knob and pulled, but it was still locked! Darn it!

Again the voices rose in volume. There, she thought, I can almost make out what they are saying. Pressing her ear to the crack in the door frame, she held her breath and listened...

A deep booming voice echoed from down the hall, "I done told you several times! That gold is on that Ranch! We just have to find it. The old man refused to tell me, kept saying he didn't know what I was talking about. Hell, even when I threatened to shoot him, he wouldn't tell me! Then he just turned his horse and started riding away, so I shot him! Dang ole man anyway! It was his own dang fault for not telling me where it was hid! But, now I have this deed to the ranch. If he didn't get it registered then we can claim the ranch and look for the gold without anyone being the wiser!"

Another voice broke in, "well, there's always a chance that maybe he really didn't know about the gold. What if your ole grandpa just thought it was on the Diamond Ranch? Hell! Are you even sure his partner was really a relative of those ranchers? That stage robbery was a long time ago, you know?

Then another man's voice broke in, somewhat softer in volume, "You don't even have any proof the gold was even stolen by your grandpa!

I heard they were caught and those that didn't hang went to Leavenworth Prison in Kansas for life!"

Again, the deep booming voice cut in, "My grandpa said it was in a large freight box with Wells Fargo painted on it. The gang he was with held up the stagecoach, rode for a couple days and nights then buried the gold. They were to meet back there in six months when things had settled down. But they were caught just a few hours after they left there, down by Broken Bow. Three of them were sent to prison down in Leavenworth, for twenty years. The other two were hung for shooting the stage driver. Grandpa was the only survivor from prison, but he was sure of where they had buried it. I don't care if he was old and feeble minded at the end. He wouldn't lie to me about the gold!"

Now the softer voice spoke again, "But, what if he got the name of the ranch wrong?"

Boomer blasted again, "Listen, you idiots. I know what my grandpa said on his deathbed. He said "Find the gold, Diamond Ranch, in the Hills. Now, the Sandhills are the only "hills" I've ever heard tell of and that's what this place is! I've been a whole lotta places and ain't never seen country like this. I know this is the right place! Hell, besides there's only one Diamond Ranch in the whole blasted Territory! Why, are you all being so dang stubborn?"

Another man cut in, "Well, just seems like we been up to a lot of work and no results! What about the ranch? If they give us the gold, what are you gonna do with the ranch? And speaking of such things, just what do you have in mind for the girl?"

Boomer guffawed, "I'll sell the ranch! Someone in Kansas City is always looking to buy land out here. And as for that girlie, why, she's our Ace in this card game. We're gonna swap her for the gold! Her daddy, the sheriff will be able to convince that rancher's son to help him out. We just need to send a ransom note and sit back and relax! A couple of the boys can hang around town and keep tabs on the sheriff and him, see when and where they go to get the gold. Then, one of the boys can ride back and let us know and we'll follow them to the gold. We'll take care of both of them, grab the gold and head south to Mexico. We can live like kings in old Mexico! Senoritas! Tequila! Whooeee!

Again the soft voice broke in……..."But, what about the girl? Are you going to kill her, too?"

"Naw, not her!" Boomer said, "We're gonna sell her to some of those outlaw comancheros down by the Mexican border. They're crazy about pretty women! They'll pay dearly for her!" There were several hoots and hollers and then sounds drifted away.

Gasping, after hearing that last statement, April pulled back from the door, holding her hand over her mouth. Not knowing whether to rant and rave at the men or to cry. This predicament was starting to get really scary. What was she going to do? These men planned to kill her father and some rich rancher's son, then, sell her to the commancheros? Good Heavens!

She had heard a story at school about the commancheros, a band of them had attacked a wagon train headed to California territory. She knew that she did not want to wind up with them. She had to get away. Think! There had to be a way out! Patrick always had found a way out of the sticky messes that they had gotten into! Oh, how she wished he was here!

Eyes tearing, but trying not to cry, April looked around the shabby little room, hoping to see, by some miracle, a way out. Looking toward the window, she could tell that it was getting to be almost sundown. There was very little light showing through the cracks in the boards now. It would be dark out soon and though it would be good cover to escape under, but she had no idea where they were.

She had been out cold when she was ferreted away from her home. She didn't even know what direction from Brewster that they had traveled. She was sincerely hoping that by this time, her father knew she was missing and was out looking for her. She had told him that morning, she would be fixing supper and would make extra for Doc Therien and Patrick. He would have expected to find her at home with supper on the table that first night, now it was two days past. Surely, he'd know something was terribly wrong if she wasn't at home, wouldn't he? If, she could only go back to that morning! And start the day all over again.

Slowly she walked over to the bed. Laying back down she started crying. Woefully, wishing she could have changed how she had rushed out of the Doctor's house, not waiting for her father to walk her home. Then, that brought thoughts of Patrick to mind and that made her cry even harder, till finally, she cried herself to sleep.

CHAPTER 11

It was around midnight, when she was startled awake, feeling like she was being smothered by a great woolly dog! It was a great hairy man beast reeking of whiskey, which was hugging and slobbering kisses on her. She released a bloodcurdling scream and swung her right arm, connecting hard with that someone's head! Frightened out of her wits, she struggled to free herself from the foul smelling man, screaming and yelling some very colorful words she didn't even realize she knew.

Suddenly, she was released and fell backwards onto the bed. Then, she heard sounds like someone was being clobbered over the head and drug out the door. In a few seconds, a dim light threw long shadows through the doorway. Entering the room, the old man who had brought her food and water earlier that day, looked at her and asked, "You okay, missy?"

"Yes, I think so. Who was that awful man?" April asked, as she stood by the bed, clutching her hands together, half frightened out of her wits.

"Don't you worry, he won't be bothering you no more." The old man said, as he shouldered his way out the door closing it behind him. Thankfully, he had left the lamp on the trunk, so it wasn't pitch black in the room anymore.

April looked at the closed door, shaking as the panic set in. What was she going to do? She couldn't even protect herself from those men. What if they overpowered the old man and got to her! She had to get out of here immediately! Throwing her hair back, she quickly braided it, tore a strip from her skirt and bound the end of the braid so it wouldn't come unraveled.

Quickly walking over to the trunk, she moved the lamp to the floor and opened the lid slowing trying to be as quiet as she could. Kneeling down, she silently prayed as she quickly sorted through the contents. There was an old hairbrush and mirror. Next, she found a couple of old hat pins stuck in a piece of leather that was folded over. Setting them aside, she continued, hoping beyond hope that there might be a gun in this old trunk. Ha! Fat chance, she thought. She continued searching through the items, reaching the bottom layer of contents. As she picked up an old rolled up shirt, a sheathed hunting knife rolled free, dropping to make a dull thudding sound. Quickly, she grabbed it and held it close to her chest, hoping no one had heard the noise. Thank you, God, she prayed.

Holding it up, she pulled the knife from the old leather sheath. It was old, but very well made, with a long wide blade that winked at her in the soft light. This will have to work since there's no gun, she thought as she rose to her feet and headed toward the window.

Stopping abruptly, she whirled around and went to the door and placed her ear against the wood, listening intently. It sounded like the men were still drinking and playing cards, for she could hear talking and occasional laughter. Trying to remain calm, she went back over to the window. Shoving the edge of the blade under the edge of the outer board, April pried slowly, continuing to slide the knife further under the board as it loosened up from the nails. Eventually, she was able to pull the board loose completely on one end and push it aside. It made a squeaking sound as it turned on the nail that was still holding the top end. Pausing, she held her breath, listening to see if anyone might come to see what the noise was about. After a moment or two, she continued with the next two lower boards. As she pushed the last one aside, she swung her leg up and started to step through the opening, when it dawned on her that she didn't know what was outside that window!

Cautiously backing up, April picked up the lamp and held it at the opening, looking out and down. Thank God! The ground was only about three or four feet down from the window. I shouldn't break anything, she thought, as she set the lamp back down on the floor. I'll just grab this knife and this old shirt, in case I need them. She quickly went over to the pitcher and drank a couple of deep swallows, not knowing how long it would be before her next drink of water. There was no way for her to take any water with her. She would just have to do without for awhile, but hopefully they weren't that far from town. Grabbing the knife she tied it up the best she could in the old shirt, then going to the opening she dropped the bundle to the ground. It made a soft plunk! Losing no time, she put her left leg through and gingerly set her bottom on the narrow ledge, pulling her right leg up and over the lip of the window, said a silent pray, and dropped down to the soft ground.

Well, that was as easy as pie, she thought as she straightened up from her crouch. She grabbed the pack she had thrown out the window first and tied it around her waist. She glanced around, waiting for her eyes to adjust to the darkness. After a few moments, April noted there was a small barn to her left, with a corral of several shadowy forms moving around, which she was sure were horses. Silently, she made her way over to the corral, finding a post with a bridle hanging over the top. Great, she thought! This is really going to be much easier with a horse! Now, I just have to get one of them to let me get this bridle on it!

It took several minutes of cooing and coaxing, before she was able to get a tall blaze faced sorrel to come close enough to get an arm around his neck when he dipped his head. Stretching up on her toes she was able to get the bit in his mouth and pull the headstall over his ears. The gelding was the tallest she had ever seen and hoped she would be able to mount him. Leading the sorrel over to the fence, she slid the ends of the poles out of the framework, as quietly as she could, then walked to the other end and pulled the other ends out of that post.

Tugging the reins she led the sorrel over to the fence, crawled up on to the very top rail and pulled herself onto the horse's back. Making sure her bundle was secure around her waist she urged the horse over the poles laying on the ground. He didn't exactly bulk, but then again, he certainly was taking his own sweet time!

Just as his rear foot cleared the last pole, she heard a ruckus at the house. Grabbing a handful of the sorrel's mane, she kicked his flanks with all her might. Wham! It felt like she was being shot out of a cannon. She struggled to stay upright and on the lunging horse's back. At her kick in his sides, the sorrel had exploded into instant motion, letting out a squeal like he had been poked with a pitchfork! His sudden movement caused the other horses to shy away from him, but they quickly circled back, seeing the opening in the fence, and followed him out of the corral. Within seconds they were all running hell bent for election!

Yells could now be heard behind them as April rode for her life. The gang opened fire, but were actually shooting over her head, for the outlaws didn't want to hit any of their horses.

April suddenly realized that the outlaws needed the horses to pursue her. If only there was a way she could get all the horses to continue to follow her horse far away from here. She hadn't really taken time to think her escape through all the way, which she hated to admit to herself. She only knew that she had to get away from those men, they were very dangerous and she was very scared.

After the first few minutes of running from the corral and the shots were no longer being fired at them, the sorrel slowed slightly, but kept to a ground-eating lope. The rest of the horses fanned out on either side of him and kept pace. It seemed that the big sorrel knew where he was going. It made April feel like she was being protected by warriors as she looked at the racing horses flanking both sides of the sorrel. After a few miles of running in the moonlight across the hills, she pulled the sorrel down to a walk. April decided she needed to give him and the other horses a breather, so she rode up the next hill slowly. As she reached the top, the other horses raced up circling around her and the big sorrel. The tall, well muscled gelding, tossed his head and nickered at his friends.

"Well," she stated to the milling animals, "I'm not alone now! I've got you, my own gang, for protection!" Strangely, as if understanding what she had just said, some of the horses tossed their heads, nickering softly. Oh, she thought, it's as if they understood and would keep her safe!

While the horses rested, April gazed upward at the moon and the millions of stars. She was able to determine that she had been heading due east. Gazing down from the hill into the valley, she could see a few twinkling lights off in the distance. Was it campfires or could it be Brewster? Well, she thought, there's only one way to find out!

She nudged the sorrel down the hill at a walk, while he tossed his head and nickered at his friends, drawing them closer to him, as if he was commanding them to guard the girl on his back. April reached down and patted the sorrel and thanked him, telling him when they returned to town, she would feed him apples to his hearts' delight. When he tossed his head in response, she was positive that he had understood her.

Lacing her fingers in his mane she urged him into a comfortable lope toward the flickering lights and what she hoped was home.

CHAPTER 12

Where in the hell is that girl? What direction had they taken her? Patrick wondered as he held onto the headboard of the bed, pulling himself upright. Enough was enough! He refused to lay here doing nothing while he knew April was in danger! Trouble sure does seem to follow her around, he thought. Life with her would never be dull, that was for sure!

Dull? Now, where did that idea come from? She was just the Sheriff's daughter. He only felt responsible because of that, nothing else!

Doc Therien had made him stay in bed for the couple days, saying if he kept moving, he would tear open the wound preventing it from healing. Meanwhile, Sheriff Hayes had rounded up several men and was out searching for his daughter.

Two days previous, after that "embarrassing moment" with April, Sheriff Hayes had came running back into Patrick's room less than thirty minutes after leaving, stating that April was not at home, that he had found her sunbonnet laying by the side of the road in front of the Church.

Doc Therien came in after hearing the ruckus and asked, "Did you check the house? Maybe she just went for a walk. You know she might be checking out the washhouse or the other out buildings?"

"No," Sheriff Hayes panted, " I checked the house and the barn, even the horses are all there. She wasn't anywhere to be found. I know she's not out for a walk because she had plans to fix supper and bring some back over here for you and Patrick."

Swinging his legs out of bed, Patrick pulled himself upright. "I'll get dressed and go with you".

"I can't let you do that." Doc Therien said as he rushed to catch Patrick's arm and force him to sit back down on the bed. "You aren't going anywhere today! I'm going to stir up something to help you heal faster," he said as he turned to the table where his doctor's bag sat. Grabbing a water glass, he dumped some powdery substance in, added water and stirred vigorously. Walking back over to Patrick, he handed the glass to him ordering him to drink it all.

Glaring at Doc, Patrick upended the glass, swallowed the vile mixture, grimaced and handed it back. "What is that stuff? It tastes terrible!"

Doc Therien, smiled at him, "Just something to make you feel better in no time. Now let's get a plan to find April."

The three men put their heads together, establishing what may have happened to the Sheriff's daughter and how to find her.

Patrick said, "I wonder if the gang is seeking revenge for our escape? They must have followed us back to Brewster. Waiting and watching until they saw April alone, then they kidnapped her. But, I don't know why they would take her."

Sheriff Hayes added, "I stopped by the livery and told Edward to saddle up some horses. He was going to roundup some more men to ride with me. We'll be heading out soon as I get back over there. I just wanted to give you a heads up in case any of that gang comes looking for you." He handed Patrick a pistol, "and I'll put this rifle by your bed, too, so it'll be handy, just in case."

And that was the last thing Patrick remembered, till early the next morning. Doc's remedy had worked like a charm! It had kept him in bed, not moving and danged if he didn't feel a lot better. The day passed without word from the Sheriff or any of the posse. No riders returned. Patrick was on pins and needles all day, wondering what direction the kidnappers had gone and if Sheriff Hayes had been able to pick up a trail of April's kidnappers. He wanted to get out of this blasted bed and help look for April.

That night, Patrick tossed and turned, getting little sleep. Dreams, like scattered bits and pieces, jumped around in his head. He was really worried about April and what could befall her at the hands of that ruthless gang.

Early, the second morning, Patrick had managed to pull himself out of bed and was almost on his feet when Doc Therien came in the room, pushed him back onto the bed and scowled, "And just where to you think you're going, young man?"

"Doc, I can't just lay here while April's in trouble," Patrick snapped, feeling light headed even as he lay back down.

"You eat some breakfast this morning, then I'll let you sit up in a chair for awhile", Doc said, as he checked the bandage on Patrick's side.

"But I need to help. She could be in serious trouble with those outlaws. We got away from them a couple times, so they won't be taking any chances with her this time. And you know damn well they wouldn't take her for no good reason! And what if the Sheriff can't locate them?"

Doc Therien patted Patrick's shoulder and nodded his head, "I know you're worried about the girl, son, we all are. Sheriff Hayes will find her and bring her back home. In the meantime, you have to stay in bed and rest. Heck, when she gets home, you can hogtie her to your chair and watch out for her. But right now, listen to me and get some rest. You have to heal and get your strength back before you go gallivanting out of here. I have a feeling that you'll have your hands full with that girl! She sure does beat all I ever seen! Riding all that way dressed like a boy and by herself. She's a pistol alright!"

Patrick was only hearing about half of what Doc was saying. His mind was drifting off and once again he was thinking of April. He wondered if she was totally scared to death, screaming, crying and carrying on like some women tend to do or trying to escape from her kidnappers. He wished he was with her, protecting and helping her. Heaven knew she definitely needed some protecting! Trouble followed that girl like bees on honey!

But he did have to chuckle, when he thought of her in this predicament. She was probably giving her captors such a difficult time that they might turn her loose, just to get rid of her! She certainly was a little spitfire!

Breaking into his thoughts, he heard Doc Therien speak again, "You need to rest and to get better. Here, drink this," handing Patrick a glass with another medical concoction in it.

As Patrick drank the vile stuff, he sputtered, "Just what is that stuff? Are you trying to kill me or cure me?"

"Finish it," Doc said, as he put his hand on the bottom of the glass tipping it back to Patrick's mouth. "No, it won't kill you, just help you sleep. When you wake up, I'll let you get out of this bed and you can sit up in the chair for awhile. Then, we'll see how you handle that." Doc turned and put the glass on the night stand and returned the bottle of medicine back into his black bag. "I'll let you have some quiet now and come back to check on you in a while."

As the Doctor left the room, Patrick grimaced as he sat sideways on the edge of the bed, forcing his body to do his bidding. Holding onto the headboard, he was able to maintain a standing position. After a couple minutes he worked his way along the wall to the cabinet where his clothes were.

He pulled open the cabinet door, where indeed he found his clothing, washed and folded neatly. Tossing his denim pants and cotton shirt over to the bed, he closed the door and took a deep breath. This was certainly a lot harder than he thought it oughta be!

Being cautious, he followed along the wall with one hand till he was back at the bed where he sat back down, wondering what had happened to all his strength. Maybe, if he just rested for a few minutes, he would feel stronger and then he could get dressed. Lying back down, Patrick was not even aware that he had fallen asleep as soon as his head hit the pillow.

Several hours later, Patrick awoke, to find the Sheriff and the Doctor entering his room. Glancing over to the curtained window, he saw that it was now dark outside. How could he have slept all day? It had to be that concoction that Doc Therien had made him drink earlier this morning! Sitting bolt upright, he gained the attention of the two men.

"Good, you're awake," Doc said. "How are you feeling, son?"

Patrick glared at the Doctor. "What did you put in that drink this morning? I've been out all day!"

Doc smiled back at him. "Yes! And I'm sure it did wonders for you! So, tell me how you feel?"

Patrick thought about how he had wasted the whole day sleeping when he should have been out looking for April. Then, slowly it dawned on him that he wasn't quite as weak feeling or as tired. "Okay, so maybe I do feel better. Now, can I get out of this damn bed and do something?"

"Sure. The café is sending over some supper for you. It should be here any minute. Have you got your appetite back?" Doc asked.

"Actually, I'm starving to death!" Patrick admitted. Looking over at the Sheriff, he stated grimly, "You didn't find her, did you."

The Sheriff sadly shook his head, "We followed a trail heading south down toward McMillan's, but lost it at the river. No signs on the other side, we checked for a mile up and down each side. I'm afraid that they must have split-up and went two separate directions. Some of the men camped at the river and will continue searching for a trail at daylight."

I came back with the rest to try to find another trail. We'll start looking again at daylight, back where I found her bonnet by the Church.

As the Sheriff sat down in the wooden chair by the bed, his face was showing the signs of defeat at not finding his daughter. Patrick understood the Sheriff's feelings, because he was feeling pretty helpless about his father's senseless death and now April's disappearance. "We'll find her, but she's a tough cookie, sir. I'm sure she'll be okay, you know she's a spit-fire. She won't let them take advantage of her!" Now, Patrick thought to himself, who am I trying to convince him or me?

Footsteps were coming down the hall, Doc Therien spoke up, "Here comes your supper now, Patrick. You eat up and you'll feel good as new." "I ordered steak and potatoes, that'll get your blood built back up. Seems like you lost an awful lot of it before you made it back to town."

Patrick didn't care to think that many days backward. He was thinking of tomorrow and continuing the search for April. His days were running together. How long had she now been missing? Was she alright? He had to help find her. Maybe Red Feather would change his mind and come back soon. Admitting to himself that his friend, Red Feather could out-track him, Patrick knew that he would help find April. But how long would it be before he came back to town? It might take too much time if he waited for Red Feather. Patrick decided he would go himself, at daybreak.

"Sheriff, you go get some rest, and in the morning, you bring my horse with you. I'm going," Patrick stated, defying the Doctor to disagree.

At that moment, Blaine, Tracy Bradley's son, from Uncle Buck's café walked through the doorway bearing a tray that wafted aroma's that had Patrick's stomach growling! Handing the tray to Doc, the youth grinned a howdy to Patrick, "Ma says you are to eat all of this and if you want more, I can bring another steak." He nodded to the older men and was gone in an instant.

"Here, you're going to need this if you think you're riding tomorrow," Doc said as he placed the heavily laden tray of delicious smelling food on Patrick's lap.

Sheriff Hayes rose from his chair, "Okay, Patrick. If Doc says you can ride, I'll bring your horse in the morning. What do you say Doc?"

Doc Therien, shook his head, "You'll be going against my better judgment, but you're going to go anyway, aren't you?" The Doctor looked at Patrick with a look of fatherly concern, waiting for the response he knew Patrick would give.

"You're damn right, I'm going!" Patrick shot back, then started in on the meal from the café.

Doc Therien and the Sheriff left the room, their voices dwindling as they walked down the hallway. Doc was telling the Sheriff that he thought Patrick would be okay riding, but to keep a watchful eye on the stubborn fool. Sheriff Hayes agreed with the Doctor that Patrick was definitely stubborn, but he really needed his help to find April.

Finishing off the filling and delicious meal, Patrick set the tray on the nightstand next to the bed. Sighing with satisfaction at feeling better and being well fed, Patrick lay back onto his pillows, already planning the search they would continue in the morning for April. He said a little prayer that God would keep her safe till he could reach her. Then, he had plans to turn that girl over his knee again!

CHAPTER 13

It seemed like only a few minutes ago that he had been making plans for finding April, when he found himself suddenly awakened from a sound sleep. Had there been a noise? Had he been asleep long? The kerosene lamp was now out and the only illumination was the moonlight from a full moon falling through the open window. There was a slight breeze blowing, softly rippling the curtain panels at the sides of the window. Taking a deep breath, Patrick slowly let it out, listening again for whatever had awakened him. It was silent, not even the crickets were singing. There, he heard it again, a familiar sound...........it was running horses! Throwing back the blankets, Patrick stood, suddenly feeling stronger than he had in days. Grabbing his pants, that were still lying on the end of the bed, he pulled them on. Reaching, he pulled his boots from under the edge of the bed and shoved his feet in without waiting to put on his socks. Someone was coming into town riding hell-bent or was it a stampede? But, who in hell would stampede through town in the middle of the night? The gang? Picking up the pistol off the dresser and grabbing the rifle by the door, Patrick hurried out the door and down the hallway. His mind was racing. Had the gang came back to town? Pumping the lever to load a shell into the chamber of the rifle, Patrick stepped out of the front door of the Doctor's office and into the middle of the dark street. It was illuminated by only a couple of kerosene lanterns hanging from poles at the end of the street. Although the moonlight was bright enough to outline what his eyes did not believe they were seeing. At a full gallop, coming directly at him, was April on his father's large sorrel gelding, Sundance. They were closely followed by a herd group of riderless horses, guessing there was over a dozen.

Never, in his entire lifetime would he ever forget this sight. She was beautiful, he thought. With her hair streaming behind her, her eyes and face were shining as she smiled and rode on, directly toward him. This is what it should feel like, he thought. Now knowing, he was a goner. Hook, line and sinker for the girl!

Skidding to within a few feet of Patrick, the sorrel horse carrying April stopped and reared up, nickering and pawing the air as if to announce their arrival. April clung easily to his back, her hands entwined in his mane, the pair looking as if they were one being. Their fluid movements were in time with each other, an understanding of two souls, in silent communication.

Patrick dropped the guns and stepped forward just as the sorrel landed back on earth. Reaching up, April fell into his arms, laughing and crying at the same time. They clung to each other, sending their emotions to each other without uttering a word.

Within a few minutes of the herd's arrival, several people had shown up in the street, wanting to see what was going on. All were trying to ask April questions on where she had been and if she was alright. Her father, Sheriff Hayes arrived out of breath, having run all the way from his house to the main street. April ran flying into his arms. Tears ran down his face as he held her close and looked at Patrick over her head, conveying all his love for his daughter in that one look.

Patrick nodded, signaling the Doctor to go with the Sheriff and April. As they walked away, Patrick said to the gathering crowd, "Okay, everything is going to be fine, but I could use some help putting these horses into the corral over by the livery". Several men stepped forward to help head the horses into the corral, with Patrick leading the way, walking with his hand on the neck of his father's spirited sorrel. Before he shut the gate, he patted Sundance's neck and thanked him for delivering April back to him. The sorrel tossed his head in acknowledgment, softly nickering his answer back. Patrick had only seen one other horse communicate like that. His stud, Dew-Bars, seemed to have that same uncanny ability. It had saved his life more than once.

As the rest of the town folk went back home to their beds, Patrick headed back to the Doctor's office. He needed to finish dressing then go check on April. He didn't think he should leave her unguarded after this last incident. He knew the gang would try to even the score. It was just a matter of time. He was already running ideas through his mind for a plan to protect her. But he needed to find out more about why the gang had been after her in the first place.

He would go see Francis Doud, a retired rancher and a good neighbor, who had known his grandfather. Maybe he would be able to fill in the background and help make sense of this whole mess before someone else was killed by this gang besides his father. Because now, Patrick was sure they were the ones who had shot his father in the back and stolen the deed to the ranch.

Francis Doud and his wife, Katie, were retired school teachers from the local country school who had been ranchers and close friends and neighbors of the Diamond family. Francis had known Patrick's grandfather when they were both in their young and foolish days as he liked to call it.

Patrick would head out there in the morning, but he was taking care of the situation with April tonight. Back in the Doctor's office, Patrick wasted no time. He finished dressing, this time putting on his socks and shirt. Strapping on his gun belt, he felt better than he had in days. He dropped the borrowed pistol into the holster and picked up the rifle as he headed out the door. As he walked, he was ticking off possible solutions to the problems of dealing with the gang. For he was certain it would only be a short time before they came back to town and his first thought was to protect April. To do that, he was going to get her out of town as soon as possible.

Stopping by the livery, Patrick saddled up Dew-Bars, leading him out of the barn before mounting. The big sorrel, Sundance, was agitated and running the fence line of the corral. When Patrick turned to ride away, the sorrel ran at the fence, easily clearing the top pole which was over five foot. Hearing the horse land behind him, Patrick turned back his stud, laughing, "What's the matter big fella, don't want to get left behind?" The sorrel tossed his head and nickered in response. "Okay, come on, you can go!"

Dew-Bars, being a stud, normally didn't tolerate geldings very well. He stomped and danced around, snorting his displeasure of another male even though he knew Sundance. Patrick patted his neck, soothing him and said, "It's okay, he's gonna help us out. Don't be so jealous! Come on, time's a wasting!" Touching his heels to Dew-Bars, they wheeled and headed to Sheriff Hayes' house.

The house was lit up when Patrick stepped down from the saddle and up onto the front porch. He left the reins on the saddle horn, knowing he didn't have to tie up his mount. The sorrel stood obediently beside Dew-Bars, waiting without a rein or any rope to tether him.

Knocking on the front door, Patrick could hear voices, probably coming from the kitchen, hollering to come on in, that the door was open. Pushing down on the latch, he pushed open the door and stepped into the front room. Before he could turn to shut the door, April ran into the room and hugged him. Hugging her in return, he then gently set her apart from him, just as her father walked in with Doc Therien. The Sheriff looked as if he had aged ten years and Doc didn't look much better.

Knowing something was up, Patrick looked askance at them both without saying a word. Sheriff Hayes took April's arm and walked her over to the sofa in front of the fireplace. "Here now girl, you set down and rest, you have had enough excitement for awhile."

Doc gave Patrick the high sign to come with him, back to the kitchen, while saying, "We'll bring the coffee into the living room so we can all sit down."

Once in the kitchen, Doc turned to Patrick, glancing toward the doorway they had just walked through, "I think we better get some more men, I think the gang will show up here soon, looking for her." He then filled Patrick in on what April had overheard at the abandoned house before her escape. "I don't know how she got away, but I can bet they are very angry that she got away and left them with no horses. If they can get more, they'll come after her, I'm sure of it!"

"I was thinking almost the same thing, but not the more men idea", Patrick said as he picked up a potholder and lifted the hot coffeepot from the back of the cook stove.

"I'm going to take her out to the Ranch, I have enough men there to keep a sharp eye out for the gang and I'll send in some men to help out here in town. I need you to send a telegram to the US

Marshall's office and see what you can find out about a robbery around the time of my grandfather's younger years, before he married my grandmother. I think it may have been a train robbery or a stage coach, something that had something to do with a great deal of gold and Wells Fargo. You tell them to hurry, then send a couple of rider's to the ranch to let me know what you find out. I don't want anyone traveling alone or unarmed. Tell the rider's to be very cautious of any strangers, even if it's only a couple men. In the morning, I am going to talk with Francis Doud, he knew my grandfather and may be able to give me more information on what this mess is all about."

Doc set coffee cups on a tray with some bread and cheese, and headed for the doorway. "I'll make my excuses and go send that telegram right now. You send the Sheriff on over to my office. We'll take care of getting things ready here in town. When are you planning on leaving for the ranch?"

"As quick as she eats this bread and cheese and drinks a little coffee", we need all the time we can get before the gang shows up and figures out we aren't here anymore." Patrick followed along behind the Doctor as they took the coffee and food into the front living room.

Within the next half hour, April ate some food and changed back into her denim pants once again. Patrick was already outside tying a small bag onto the back of his saddle with a change of clothes for her. She now knew they would be heading to a ranch where with help, he would be able to keep the gang from getting at her again.

April still did not know that the ranch they were going to was Patrick's, she had missed out on that part of the conversation the men had had while she had changed clothes and gotten ready to leave. When she came out of the house she was happy to see the big sorrel gelding waiting beside Patrick's stallion, Dew-Bars. Patrick had not told her that it was his fathers' horse or how the outlaws had gotten him.

"Hey, there big fella, you waiting for me?" she cooed at him, petting the blazed-face horse. She pulled a piece of apple out of her pocket and fed it to the big gelding. He was a beautiful specimen of horseflesh, with as well defined muscles as the stallion next to him. His response was a soft nickering and nudge of his head against her hand.

"Well, I can't keep calling you big fella, now can I? Seems like I'll have to give you a name."

Patrick was standing beside his stallion's head watching as the two reconnected. Knowing in his heart how much his father had loved the gelding, he said, "His name is Sundance. He once belonged to someone I know, who, I'm sure wouldn't mind you having him."

"Oh, what happened to him?" April asked hesitantly, knowing instinctively that Patrick wasn't telling her everything. Reaching out her hand as the big gelding tossed his head and nickered back at them.

Looking at the big gelding, Patrick cleared his throat, "I'll tell you about him someday," leaving the topic for a later time and place.

"Okay, Sundance, why don't you and I take this girl where she'll be safe?" Patrick said as he lifted April up to the gelding's back. He then mounted Dew-Bars and they headed out of town toward his Ranch.

CHAPTER 14

Patrick figured they should arrive at the ranch in the next couple hours with steady riding. They had stopped once at the river to water the horses and continued on through the star flung night over the rolling Sandhills toward his home.

Patrick had no intention of letting April know that the place they were headed for was actually his home, the ranch where he had been born and raised. Maybe sometime after this matter with the gang was settled, he would be able to tell her everything. But first, they needed to protect her from the gang and find out what they could about any stolen gold and what it had to do with his fathers' death and the ranch.

April had not complained once about the pace he had set when they left Brewster and headed out to the ranch. The day was just dawning as they came over the last hill. Patrick pulled up Dew-Bars and paused, gazing down at his home.

April, sighed and said, "Oh, Patrick, it's such a beautiful place", you sure they won't mind me coming out here?"

Patrick, turned and said, "No, they'll be happy to help out." "I'll introduce you to Mrs. Akin, the housekeeper and then head over to the Doud place and see what I can find out."

Together, they admired the beautiful layout of the Diamond Ranch. The buildings and yard were bordered by tree strips that Patrick's grandfather had planted when he had homesteaded the place. The pine trees were now full grown and provided homes to a multitude of wildlife. The corrals were quartered off from the barn with a large circular area for breaking horses and working cattle. There were a few smaller pens graduating off from the main corral to keep a small number of cattle in for doctoring or sorting.

To the west of the barn was a fenced pasture where two milk cows grazed. They faithfully provided the ranch with fresh milk, cream and butter for the ranch hands and household.

As they rode down the hill into the yard, a ranch hand appeared from the wide barn door, ready to take their horses. Patrick dismounted from Dew Bars, and turned to help April as she slid from the big gelding's back. Sundance had kept steady pace with Dew Bars all the way to the ranch and Dew-Bars never once nipped or bullied him.

April had not asked whose ranch this was, but as she looked around her, she thought maybe it was where Patrick had once worked. It was a beautiful home, she thought. A place one would be proud of.

As the cowboy lead Dew-Bars into the barn, Sundance nickered at her, so she kissed his soft nose, patted his neck and said, "it's okay, go ahead and I will see you later." He turned and walked into the barn following the stallion.

"Amazing," Patrick said, "I thought only Dew-Bars understood people."

April, sighed, "It is amazing, isn't it? I feel as if he can read my mind."

Patrick stated, "Well, him and Dew-Bars will get some feed and a well deserved rubdown for their efforts this morning. Let's head up to the house," and held out his hand.

April smiled up at him and placed her small hand into his strong one and they walked together toward the large house. It was surrounded by a covered porch that lent a person shade all day, not depending which side of the house you were on. Wide steps lead up to the front door, allowing them to walk side by side.

Just as they approached, the screen door was opened and a youthful middle-aged woman stepped out and started to say, "Hello, Mr. D...", when Patrick cut her off with a slight shake of his head.

He quickly said to her, "Mrs. Akin, I would like you to meet April Hayes, the sheriff's daughter. He was wondering if she might stay here a few days? I'll explain everything later, okay?"

"Sure, you just come on in with me and I'll get you something to eat and drink. I'll bet you're parched from your ride out from town," Mrs. Akin said, wondering all the while what this young girl was doing with her boss, Mr. Diamond. She wondered what had happened since she had seen him just a few days ago?

April looked up at Patrick, he nodded and said, "Go on ahead, I'll be back in awhile." With that, he turned and headed down the steps toward the bunk house. Mrs. Akin led April on into the cool interior of the ranch house and was promising April some breakfast of ham and eggs as April's stomach growled at the thought.

At the bunkhouse, the foreman and ranch hands were finishing their breakfast when Patrick entered. The cook handed him a plate of food and a cup of coffee. As Patrick ate his meal, he outlined what had been happening over the last few days. He instructed Chris the foreman, to place guards around the ranch quarters and some a half mile out from the buildings to keep any unwanted visitors from approaching the ranch. He picked out a dozen cowboys to head back into town to help out the Sheriff. They finished their breakfast, buckled on gun belts, grabbed rifles and headed for the barn to saddle up their horses for the ride into Brewster.

When they were heading out, Patrick saddled up a fresh horse and headed south toward the Doud place. He was hoping to find out if Francis might know something about the old robbery and the gang that had done it.

Arriving at the Doud ranch, Patrick rode up to a hitching rail in front of a fenced yard that was surrounded with newly planted flower beds.

Dismounting, he tied his quarter horse, Chuck, to the rail then passed through the swinging gate. He walked up the stone path leading up to the front porch of the house. Just as he approached the porch, the front door swung opened and both Francis and Katie Doud stepped out to greet him.

"Why land sakes!" Katie said as she gave Patrick a quick hug and kissed his cheek. "We were wondering when you'd come by. How are you doing, son?"

Francis shook Patrick's hand and motioned to a pair of rockers on the front porch. As Patrick sank into the comfortable old chair, he sighed, "I hate to say it, but I've been better. I came over to see if you remember anything about an old robbery and some gold back when my Granddad was young and first came to this area."

Francis, thought a while, then said, "Why, now that you mention it, I do recall there was a big ruckus about the Sheriff from Broken Bow hanging some men who robbed a stage or train or something, but I don't think they recovered any gold. Why do you ask?"

"Because I think that's why my dad was shot in the back. Apparently, one of the original gang had a grandson who he may have told about the gold. And Sheriff Hayes and I think he's come looking for it." Patrick continued by telling the Doud's what had transpired over the last week. Katy and Francis were aghast that something like this had befallen their neighbor, whom they had known all his life.

"What can we do to help?" Francis asked.

"Do you have any idea where they may have buried the gold, if they did bury it on the ranch?" Patrick asked. "Was there any landmarks at that time that may be gone now that the gang used as a site?"

"Well, now there used to be a place down by the Loup River that was known for an Indian burial ground. But I don't think there's much left to identify it anymore." Francis was lost in thought for a few moments then said, "There was this big old cottonwood tree just west of the grounds and I think it's still standing. It's been hit by lightning a few times, burnt it up some, but I'm sure it's still there. I'll get a piece of paper and draw you a little map, so you know what I'm talking about." Francis rose and went into the house and soon returned with a rough sketch of the land to the south along the Loup River. He handed it to Patrick pointing out the landmarks and the where the tree was located.

"Hey, I think I know what tree you mean, but I didn't know anything about a burial ground being there. I hate to leave so abruptly, but we're running out of time," Patrick rose from his chair giving the couple his thanks. "I'll take some men and go check it out, I really appreciate the help!" He hurried back to his horse and headed back to the ranch. He would have to take a wagon and some shovels. As his side was beginning to bother him, he reckoned he'd better take a couple extra men along to help dig.

When he arrived back at the ranch he told his foreman what he needed and then headed over to the ranch house. April met him on the front porch with a questioning look on her face and a cold glass of lemonade for him.

Patrick sat down in one of the porch chairs, took the glass and drank deeply. When he told April what he had found out about where the gold might be hidden she wanted to go along, but he nixed that idea right in the bud. No way was she leaving the ranch's safety.

Just as she protested again, a wagon and four mounted ranch hands pulled up to the porch.

April said, "I am going with you," and started down off the porch.

"NO!" Patrick stated as he rose up from the chair. "You will stay here, till I get back! We won't be gone that long and we should be back by sundown."

April spun around, "You can't tell me to stay here after all that's happened! I'm going with you!"

"No, you are not!" Patrick said as he approached her on the porch steps, "you WILL stay here and stay out of trouble! Do you hear me?"

"You can't tell me what to do!" she flung at him as she took another step.

The words were no sooner out of her mouth, then Patrick grabbed her to him, kissed her firmly, and said, "You will stay HERE!" He set her down solidly on the steps and walked to the wagon. He turned and gave her a fierce look, then climbed up into the seat and took the reins and off the group went.

April was speechless! Why, that man! Who does he think he is, telling me what to do! She thought of his fierce kiss and touched her slightly bruised lips. Why couldn't he be her dream man? But he was nothing like who she was looking for! Just a cowboy with nothing. Sighing, she turned and went back into the ranch house to find Mrs. Akin and see if the housekeeper could put her to work. April needed something to keep her mind off that man!

CHAPTER 15

Within an hour or so, moving as fast as they could with the wagon, the men and Patrick arrived at the river area where the Indian burial grounds were supposed to be. As they headed up river to what was now left of the old majestic cottonwood tree, Patrick prayed they would find the gold. And do it quickly.

Francis had been right, lightning had taken a devastating toll on the old tree. No longer were there any living branches of green spreading out over the riverbank. There now stood in its place a huge partially blackened dead trunk, but it still reached into the blue sky for a good thirty foot.

The men each took a shovel and starting digging in different spots around the base of the tree, using a grid pattern so nothing would be overlooked. After about an hour of checking different spots, one of the hands hollered, "Hey, boss. I think I found something!"

All of them gathered around and starting digging out what appeared to be partially rotted wooden crates. Sure enough, they had found the gold! The men loaded the pieces of the two crates and the gold into the back of the wagon. They were excited and asked Patrick if there was a reward. He told them he was sure there would be and they could split it between them. The cowboys hooted and hollered as they headed back to the ranch.

When they returned, Mrs. Akin and April were waiting impatiently, to say the least, on the front porch. Patrick told them how the men had found the gold. April wanted to leave immediately and go tell her father the good news.

"No, I'll send a couple ranch hands into town in the morning to let your father know we found the gold and to see if the posse has located the gang. I'm sure they did, given your directions. I know the US Marshall's will be there by train in a day or so. Your father had sent a telegram requesting they send several men to take the gang back. I'm sure your father has everything under control for now."

April gazed up at him, reddening slightly as she suddenly remembered the kiss and how he had taken charge of the situation earlier that morning. Oh, why did he have to be so handsome, so strong, why....and off into dreamland she went.

Patrick looked down into April's eyes, seeing her eyes darken as color rose in her face. She didn't seem to hear him as he said goodnight and turned and walked away.

He was almost to the bunkhouse before April hollered after him, "Wait! What am I supposed to do?"

Patrick turned back and said, "Go to bed. I'll see you in the morning."

Early the next morning Patrick sent the foreman and one of the ranch hands into town to check with the sheriff and let him know they had recovered the gold and find out if the sheriff had found the gang. The extra men could help out, if needed. Here at the Ranch, all they had to do was keep a sharp eye out for the outlaws and wait.

When Mrs. Akin didn't have April busy helping her in the ranch house and garden, Patrick would sit on the front porch talking with her. April talked of her childhood and what a little terror she had been for her parents. He thought he had never laughed so hard in his life when April had told him of some of her escapades and daring deeds. Why, he thought that only boys could think of such stuff! She was such an amazing girl, he thought, as he watched her smiling face when she told of another adventure of her classmates back east at boarding school. She was so full of life! It would be a lifetime effort to keep up with her, but he certainly wanted the chance.

In a few days they had word back from the sheriff. The outlaw gang had been rounded up and the papers to the Ranch recovered. The entire gang was headed for trial in Colorado. They had robbed and killed three bank employees before they had come to the Sandhills area. It was almost certain that they would all swing from a rope for that foul deed.

The US Marshalls had said yes, there was a reward and it would be equally divided among the ranch hands. Even now the cowboys were all celebrating in eager anticipation of its arrival. They were planning purchases of new gear and tack, along with more celebrating to follow up.

April now knew she could safely return back to her father and Brewster. Anticipating her future, she would still regret not getting to see Patrick everyday as she had since meeting him only a short time ago. Her last night at the ranch was spent with mixed feelings. She knew she was greatly attracted to Patrick but rationalized that it had been only chance circumstances that had thrown them together. It didn't mean anything. She had a "dream man" to find. She was sure Patrick really wasn't attracted to her; that it had all been because of their volatile personalities. Both of them were independent and strong individuals, but that was all, nothing more and nothing less. Besides he had nothing to provide for her or a family. It just wouldn't work! No way! So, she should look forward to her future, not dwell on the past.

On the morning that Patrick was to take April back to Brewster and her father, he rose early. He ate breakfast with the ranch hands, then saddled up both their horses, Dew Bars and Sundance. At least, he considered the big gelding as her horse now, knowing his father would have wanted her to have him. The big gelding and the girl seemed to share the same connection that he and Dew Bars did.

He led the horses up to the main house and left them standing untied at the hitching rail. Stepping up onto the front porch he knocked on the screen door's edge. Mrs. Akin came to the door, looking back over her shoulder, as she whispered, "Why are you knocking at your own door, Mr.Diamond?"

Patrick held his finger to his lips, then whispered back, "Is she up?"

"Yes, we were just finishing up our coffee from breakfast. Would you like a cup?"

"No, thanks, but would you ask her if she would like to go for a ride before I take her back to town?" Patrick whispered back.

"What is going on here?" the housekeeper asked quietly and totally confused at her employer's strange demeanor around this girl.

Patrick smiled in response, "Please just go ask her." Turning he headed back down the steps to the waiting horses.

In just a few moments, April came hurrying out of the front door. Pulling up short when she saw Patrick waiting patiently by the horses. "Mrs. Akin said you wanted to go for a ride? Where are we going? I thought you were taking me back to town this morning?"

"I am, but I want to take you for a short ride first. I have something to show you and I need to talk to you." Patrick said, grinning at her.

"Why are you grinning at me like that?" April asked, wondering what Patrick was really up to and where he might be taking her. She thought he would be anxious to take her back to her father now that everything was over. "Why can't we talk here"?

"Just come on, okay? Besides I think your horse needs the exercise." As Patrick turned to the big gelding, Sundance tossed his head and nickered at April. "See, he's asking you, too."

April looked first at Sundance then at Patrick. Men! She thought! She started down the steps wondering what in heaven's name was really going on. Even Mrs. Akin has looked like she had a secret when she delivered Patrick's message earlier. Okay, she was game! She'd go for a ride, because curiosity was getting the better of her! And she had to admit she wanted to spend as much time with Patrick as she could before she returned home to her father.

Patrick helped April up into the saddle, adjusting the stirrups to fit the length of her legs.

April watched Patrick as he mounted his stallion. Hmmm, she thought, such an attractive man. She told herself not to be silly. He was just a cowboy, nothing more.

Patrick led the way out of the ranch yard, heading toward the southwest. They rode for about a half hour, coming to the base of the biggest hill April had ever seen. She glanced at Patrick. He didn't say anything, just urged his horse up the hill. They rode quietly back and forth on the switchbacks till they reached the summit. When April pulled up beside Patrick, she sucked in her breath, "OH! Patrick, it's beautiful up here. You can see forever!"

Patrick dismounted and turned to April, holding out his arms to help her. She eagerly slid out of the saddle and when he set her feet on the ground she was standing so close to him. Patrick reached out and took one of her hands in his, raised it to his mouth and gently kissed it.

April was watching him as he raised her hand to his lips and shivered when he kissed it. She couldn't say anything, but she was hoping he would never let go of her hand! He was so... Her heart pounded, for she knew she cared deeply for this man, even if he was just a poor cowboy. She couldn't let him go! She wouldn't let him go! She blurted out, "Oh, Patrick, I-I-I love you, I don't care if you are just a broke cowboy and you don't have any money. I-I-..."

Patrick burst out laughing, he laughed so hard he had to clutch his side.

Red-faced, shaking and feeling like an utter fool, April pulled back and frowned up at him, "Why are you laughing at me? I just said I loved you, what's so danged funny about that?"

Feeling totally embarrassed and feeling the pain of being such a little fool, her ire rose to the surface. She knew she should have waited for her dream man. How could she be so impulsive! She spun on her boot heel, attempting to mount Sundance.

"Wait! Just a doggone minute," Patrick said as he grabbed her shoulders and turned her back toward the breath-taking view, then quietly said, "Honey, I'm not broke. This is my land. All of it."

Speechless, April turned back to him. She couldn't comprehend what he had just said. She looked back at the view, then at him. Finally, she was able to form words and sputtered, "Yours?"

"Yes, mine." Patrick smiled at her. Again he took her hand and held it in his large strong ones. "I want you to share it with me."

April was unable to say anymore. She just looked at Patrick. Here he was, everything she had been searching for, standing right in front of her.

"But, how could you…how did you…why didn't you?" she stammered.

Patrick pulled her gently to him. "Hush," he whispered, "I love you, April Hayes, and I intend to marry you! So just say yes and kiss me." He grinned, "You know you want to."

Her heart pounding in her ears, April lifted her soft brown eyes to gaze into his emerald green eyes. He loved her. That was all that really mattered. He *was* her Dream Man! She waited eagerly for that earth-shattering kiss that she knew was coming. Because now, she finally knew what "it" was…passionate, all consuming love!

Epilogue

Watching his love walk down the aisle with her father, Sheriff Hayes, Patrick thought his heart would burst with the love and pride he had for this firebrand woman of his. Although his best man, Red Feather, stood beside him to support him on his wedding day, Patrick could see that Red Feather only had eyes for the beautiful Montana, April's bridesmaid standing next to him. The two women had met and become very close friends over a year ago after the gang had been rounded up and sentenced. Three were hung for the killing of his father and the employees of the last robbery. The rest were sent to Leavenworth prison.

Red Feather was in his second year of medical studies back East and had just arrived back home yesterday to attend the wedding. It seemed like the whole town and countryside was here today, Patrick thought, sharing the beginning of his and April's lives together.

As Sheriff Hayes placed April's hand into Patrick's, she smiled up at him and whispered to her father, "I'll always be your little girl, Daddy! I love you!" Kissing him on his cheek she turned to the man she was to marry, Patrick Diamond, her cowboy and the love of her life.

Later after they exchanged vows and cut the cake, the couple was greeted by well-wishers and friends alike. The sounds of a violin floated on the breeze coming through the Church windows.

April was smiling up into her husband's green eyes already thinking of their honeymoon and the life they planned together.

They were looking forward to having children and raising them on the Diamond Ranch to carry on the family name and traditions.

There would never be a dull minute between them, of that she was sure. She had finally figured out how to put her daydreams to good use and was writing stories about the beautiful Sandhills and some of the adventures Patrick and her had shared. Already she had sold two of them to a publisher back East and they wanted more.

Patrick loved her stories and laughed and cried with her over some of her 'daydreams', knowing that she was full of such dreams and that he was part of them.

Watching from a side table, Doc Therien thought on how calm and quiet things had been around town lately. He smiled as Sheriff Austin Hayes stepped up beside him, "well it's certainly been a good day for a wedding, don't you think?"

Sheriff Hayes grinned back at the doctor, "You know I was just thinking the same thing. Yes, I'd wager it's going to be a good year for peace and quiet, now that those two finally have settled down!"

The sound of gunfire broke out somewhere in town. Setting his cup down, Doc Therien sighed, "Now, Sheriff, what was that you said about peace and quiet?"

Made in the USA
Charleston, SC
12 July 2014